"Everybody in town is talking about us.

It's not helping my professional image. We have to let people know we're not interested in each other," Susannah explained.

Brett laughed and moved closer to her on the bench. "You start running around protesting that we're not doing anything and everybody will assume the worst. I've found the best way to handle it is to go along with it. That way, public interest fizzles out."

"You really think so? But what about—"

"I think we'd better find out first if there's any truth behind the gossip," he interrupted.

To tell the truth, she was curious, too. Her heart was starting to pound, but she didn't turn her face away as he bent his head toward hers. Just a kiss. She could handle that.

And she really believed that until the moment Brett's lips touched hers....

Dear Reader,

Welcome to Silhouette—experience the magic of the wonderful world where two people fall in love. Meet heroines that will make you cheer for their happiness, and heroes (be they the boy next door or a handsome, mysterious stranger) who will win your heart. Silhouette Romance reflects the magic of love—sweeping you away with books that will make you laugh and cry, heartwarming, poignant stories that will move you time and time again.

In the coming months we're publishing romances by many of your all-time favorites, such as Diana Palmer, Brittany Young, Sondra Stanford and Annette Broadrick. Your response to these authors and our other Silhouette Romance authors has served as a touchstone for us, and we're pleased to bring you more books with Silhouette's distinctive medley of charm, wit and—above all—*romance.*

I hope you enjoy this book and the many stories to come. Experience the magic!

Sincerely,

Tara Hughes
Senior Editor
Silhouette Books

AMANDA LEE

Silver Creek Challenge

Published by Silhouette Books New York
America's Publisher of Contemporary Romance

To Nancy,
for helping to make Silver Creek come alive

SILHOUETTE BOOKS
300 E. 42nd St., New York, N.Y. 10017

ISBN: 0-373-08651-2

First Silhouette Books printing May 1989

Printed in the U.S.A.

Books by Amanda Lee

Silhouette Special Edition

End of Illusion #165

Silhouette Desire

Love in Good Measure #173
More Than Promises #192
Logical Choice #267
Great Expectations #347
A Place in Your Heart #425

Silhouette Romance

Silver Creek Challenge #651

AMANDA LEE

is a pseudonym for the writing team of Ruth Glick and Eileen Buckholtz, who have written more than twenty-five novels together. In addition to romance, they love books spiced with adventure and suspense. But what they consider the most fun of all is hatching their own plots and bringing memorable heroes and heroines to life. They also write under the names of Samantha Chase and Rebecca York.

SUSANNAH'S PEACH CRISP

Filling

5-7 large peaches, peeled and sliced (about 5 cups)
3 tbsp sugar
1 tbsp enriched all-purpose or unbleached white flour
½ tsp ground cinnamon

Topping

⅔ cup enriched all-purpose or unbleached white flour
½ cup light brown sugar, packed
½ cup quick-cooking rolled oats
¼ cup powdered milk, nonfat
¼ cup margarine
1 tsp ground cinnamon

Preheat oven to 350° F.

Filling: Cover bottom of a 9″ square baking pan with peach slices. Sprinkle slices with the remaining filling ingredients and stir to coat. Set aside.

Topping: In a medium-size bowl, combine all topping ingredients. Blend with fork or fingers until mixture is crumbly and margarine is incorporated. Spread over filling.

Bake 25-30 minutes or until topping is lightly browned and filling is bubbling. Serve warm. If desired, top with ice milk. Serves 5 to 7.

Chapter One

Brett Tanner tilted his chair back on its hind legs and stretched out his rangy six-foot-two frame. He knew his fellow town-council members well enough to realize that a hurricane was brewing, and it wasn't off the coast.

"I'll never be able to hold my head up in Charleston again," Bonnie Childress complained as she shifted her more-than-ample body in one of the wooden armchairs around the council table.

"It beats all, doesn't it? The first time we make the front page of the big-city paper, and it had to be something like this," Dwayne Rollins, the stocky, balding mayor of Silver Creek, commiserated.

Brett folded his corded arms across his chest. They were deeply tanned from days spent outside running his marina and taking tourists on fishing expeditions. He struggled to keep a mischievous twinkle out of his blue eyes. "You're just making a mountain out of a molehill. Let's get on with important business—like planning our Fourth of July celebration."

"Just 'cause *you* can still fit into your old high-school football uniform doesn't give you the right to make light of the issue, Brett," Bonnie scolded. Yet she couldn't hide the motherly affection in her voice. She'd sold him penny candy when he was still too short to look over the top of the counters in her general store. He'd left South Carolina in his twenties to make his fortune, but he'd come back when he'd realized that small-town values were more important than life in the fast lane.

"Reckon we'd better call this meeting to order, here," Dwayne interjected as he fanned himself with a notepad and banged his Dr Pepper can on the table for emphasis. "Bonnie, you go ahead and summarize the situation—for the record."

The rotund woman rose purposefully and drew a creased copy of Sunday's *Charleston Gazette* from her handbag. "Everybody surely knows about that blasted government study by now. Poorest fitness and nutrition habits of any town in the state. Hmph!"

There was a chorus of agreeing grunts around the room.

Bonnie dabbed the perspiration from her forehead with a tissue. The air conditioner in the council chamber broke last October, and no one had thought about it until the present unseasonable April heat wave. "We might have lived that down," she continued, "if that big-city reporter hadn't thought it was funny to label us the flab capital of South Carolina."

The sun-weathered lines at the corners of Brett's eyes crinkled as he tried to look duly concerned. "Tomorrow nobody in Charleston, or anywhere else, will even remember that article. The best thing to do is ride this out and try to keep your sense of perspective." He favored the gray-haired woman with the beguiling smile that had charmed Silver Creek's female population for the past thirty-four years. "And in case you're taking this thing personally, Bonnie, you look just fine to me."

"You say that to anything in skirts," she accused, blushing nevertheless.

"I think you're missing the seriousness of this situation," Donna Nevins spoke up from the end of the table. "That article quoted an expert from Healthways named Susannah Lindsey. She says that if we don't change our ways and eat better and get more exercise, we're going to shorten our lives." The fragile-looking redhead tucked a frizzy curl behind her ear and continued. "Worse than that, we're passing on our bad habits to our kids. As a teacher and a mother, I feel it's a shame. How about it, Doc?" She turned to the graying, bespectacled man beside her.

"I was out fishing all day Sunday and haven't seen the paper yet," Doc Crowley hedged. "Where exactly did we fall short in the evaluation?"

Donna looked pointedly at Bonnie. The older woman cleared her throat and began to read through the list. "No athletic clubs, no indoor swimming pools, no regularly scheduled exercise classes, no salad bar within the city limits, no weight-loss support groups, no city department of health, no nutrition classes for high-schoolers or adults, no health-screening programs and an alarming incidence of high blood pressure and obesity."

"Well, maybe they have a point," the doctor conceded. "A lot of people passing through my office would benefit by skipping the grits and bacon for breakfast and walking to the store instead of driving."

"I think we ought to take some steps to rectify the situation," Donna proposed as she and Bonnie exchanged conspiratorial glances. "How about a diet-and-exercise program to get everybody in town on the right track?"

"I still say there's no reason to get in a flap." Brett tipped his chair back again. "Silver Creek is a good place to live and raise your kids, no matter what some study says." He paused and gave Donna an indulgent look. "But nobody's going to object if you want to put something together."

"Now, Brett, you know I'm a day-care expert, not a nutritionist or an exercise instructor. But the paper said that Susannah Lindsey is an authority on those things. We ought to see if she'll come down here and help us."

The mayor rubbed his forehead thoughtfully. "I'm sure our treasurer has a comment on that idea. Doc, just what is our financial situation?"

"Money's real tight this year—as usual. Except for a couple of hundred in petty cash and the money earmarked to repair the air conditioner, the only funds we've got left are to pay for the Fourth of July fireworks gala."

"Well, I make a motion that we take the fireworks money and offer Miss Lindsey a job," Bonnie said.

The chairman of the fireworks committee let his chair legs drop to the wooden floor with a resounding thud. "Now wait a minute. Let's not get carried away!" Brett's rich baritone voice was still cordial. When he saw all eyes turn in his direction, he realized he'd made a mistake. The way to get what you wanted in this situation was to play it low-key and use persuasion rather than brute force. "When I was a kid, the Fourth of July fireworks were the best part of summer. I wouldn't want to have to tell my son or the other youngsters we canceled 'em,'' he said earnestly, then shook his head in sudden bemusement. ''In fact, I think I enjoy the fireworks as much as the kids.'' A quick survey of the faces around the table told him that a number of his fellow council members agreed. But that didn't mean they'd put their money on a traditional July Fourth celebration instead of some half-baked exercise hogwash.

He tried leveling with them. ''Personally, I think that article put too much emphasis on externals. All this preoccupation with dieting and exercising just makes people dissatisfied with themselves.'' He brushed a sun-streaked lock of wavy hair off his forehead. ''I'd rather judge the residents of Silver Creek on their character and behavior, not how they look. And I hope the rest of you do the same.''

''We don't have to lose our values to make a few improvements in our health,'' Donna countered firmly. ''Let's bring it to a vote.''

''Hold on a minute,'' Doc Crowley interjected. ''I want to know more about this expert before I make any decision.''

''Donna and I thought you might, Doc.'' Bonnie smiled smugly and pulled a folded sheet of paper from her purse. ''So we did a little research on Susannah Lindsey. She's a nutritionist and registered dietitian who also teaches exercise classes and does regular workout segments on one of the Atlanta TV talk shows.'' As Bonnie spoke, Donna wheeled in a cart holding a portable TV and VCR and plugged them in.

''And we have her on tape.'' Donna popped the cassette into the machine and flipped the play button with a flourish. To the beat of an energetic rock melody, the title Toning Your Tummy and Other Parts flashed on the TV screen.

Brett repressed a sigh. His mind was already made up, but he was going to have to give the women their say.

The enticing, leotard-clad instructor bounced energetically onto the screen, and despite his avowed indifference, Brett sat up a little straighter in his chair. He'd pictured Ms. Lindsey as rail-thin with no hips and no breasts. This woman was tall and trim, but she had generous curves in all the right places.

The camera zoomed in for a close-up, and he found warm brown eyes fringed with thick sable lashes focused directly on him. Susannah Lindsey's hair was long and dark, and she wore it flipped over one shoulder in a braid. "Before we get into our warm-up, take a couple of deep breaths and let them out slowly," she purred.

To his surprise, he found that he was following instructions. In reaction, his jaw firmed and he folded his arms across his chest once more.

Ms. Lindsey started her first set of warm-ups, and the camera gave him a full view again—this time from the back.

Beside him, Dwayne sucked in his breath. "If the exercise program can make my wife look like that, I'll sign on the bottom, er, dotted line right now."

Out of the corner of his eye, Brett saw Donna and Bonnie exchange smug looks.

Ms. Lindsey finished her first aerobic set. There was hardly any perspiration on her forehead. Brett couldn't say the same for his. He glanced around the room and noted that the other men were having the same reaction to the workout.

As though she was tuned in to her audience, Ms. Lindsey smiled and instructed her viewers to take their pulses. Heck, Brett guessed his was at least a hundred and fifty, and he hadn't left his chair.

"I guess that gives you a good idea of who we'd be hiring," Bonnie said as she turned off the TV and pushed the cart out of the way.

"I'll say. It ought to be illegal for a woman to look that good in a leotard." Doc Crowley chuckled.

A few minutes later the vote went for Miss Lindsey, and Brett considered what to do next. The woman *did* give a great workout. But surely town decisions should be made on more than that.

Then it suddenly occurred to him that his fireworks weren't really in much jeopardy after all. He relaxed, suppressing a grin. "I'm not going to stand in the way if you've got your hearts set on it," he acquiesced charitably.

"Then it's unanimous that we'll offer Miss Lindsey a job," the mayor summarized for the record. "Let's clear up the details so we can adjourn."

Brett was whistling as he left the council room after the meeting. He might have lost this skirmish, but he was willing to bet that he'd be enjoying a traditional Independence Day along with the rest of the town. Of course, the July Fourth entertainment was just a side issue. He really didn't want to see the town spend its hard-earned money on a fitness kick that wasn't going to improve anything except the Healthways bank account. But then, for what they were offering to pay, he figured there was about as much chance of that sexy exercise teacher actually accepting Silver Creek's offer of employment as there was of a blizzard in July.

* * *

Susannah Lindsey unfolded the rumpled map on the seat of her Skylark and traced the wiggly line that represented Route 78. It had been a fairly easy drive from Atlanta to Augusta, but the last leg of the trip had really dragged. However, she should be coming to the turn-off shortly.

It was amazing that she had been able to clear her schedule enough to take on the challenge Silver Creek had offered, she acknowledged as she readjusted the oversize designer sunglasses that protected her eyes from the slanting afternoon sun. She had managed to tape a dozen five-minute workouts for her segments on the *Larry Burns Show* and had found a substitute to handle her June and July exercise and nutrition workshops. And as if that hadn't been enough, there had been the call from the producer of *Morning USA*. They were looking for a new person to do a fitness-and-nutrition segment on the popular network show. Could she send them a proposal and a few videotapes? Of course she could. But it had taken several frantic evenings and most of the weekend to get them together.

She thought back to Jack Thompson's reaction when she'd first broached the idea of accepting the consulting job.

"Are you out of your mind?" Healthways's hard-driving vice president for operations had exclaimed. "In the first place, what they're paying won't keep you in leotards."

"I'm not doing it just for the money."

"Well, have you considered that you're going to be spending your vacation in some mosquito-infested swamp?"

"Ranting and raving won't help, Jack. I've already decided," Susannah informed him sweetly. She drew her trim, athletic body to its full five feet eight inches and stood her ground. "For your information, Silver Creek isn't a swamp. Besides, I could tell from their letter and phone calls that these people really need me." What she didn't explain to Jack was that she welcomed the change of pace from the hectic schedule she'd been keeping the last several years.

"You always were a soft touch," Jack observed. "Anyway, if we play this right, Healthways will get a lot of good publicity out of it."

"I knew your sense of social responsibility would surface sooner or later," she chided lightly.

"Don't forget you're expected back in Atlanta on the first of August. Feel free to come back sooner if you get tired of life in the backwater or if the bugs get too friendly."

She'd put on a convincing show of confidence in her decision for Jack. Privately, Susannah, a city girl born and bred, had wondered if she could handle two and a half months in such an alien environment. Still, people were people wherever they lived, she told herself. She'd sensed an openness and genuine concern in Bonnie Childress, the town's representative, that had made it impossible to say no.

Now Susannah was passing a Welcome to Silver Creek sign at the city limits and having her first look at her home base for the next two months. As she drove down Main Street, she took in what appeared to be a mixed residential and business district. The street was lined with huge oaks, a number of tidy brick residences, an insurance office and a large, white antebellum-style funeral home. At the main intersection an old stone church and gas station sat opposite each other.

The council had conveniently arranged for Susannah's lodging at a summer cottage owned by Mayor Rollins, about a mile south of town on the banks of the Edisto River. According to Bonnie's letter, the key would be under the doormat. Susannah smiled to herself. If you did that in Atlanta, you'd probably come home to find the place stripped.

Twenty-five minutes later, Susannah was standing on the screened back porch of the Rollins's weathered but inviting summer house. Although she had noticed several other houses from the road, all she could see out back was the river. The thick pines that lined the lot were as effective as a privacy fence. Susannah did a few stretching exercises to uncramp her muscles. She'd already unpacked the car and slipped into a tank top and shorts. Now it felt good to unwind.

After completing a few toe touches, Susannah padded back through the dining and sitting rooms toward the kitchen. Nora Mae Rollins had decorated the house with white wicker furniture accented with green-and-pink floral cushions and matching café curtains. The effect was airy and cheerful. And Susannah loved the back porch. It was large and wrapped around the house on three sides to catch any breezes off the water. Susannah suddenly realized she felt more relaxed than she had in years.

Maybe that explained her ravenous appetite, she thought as she entered the kitchen and took down a plate and glass from the cupboard. Nora Mae had stocked the refrigerator and pantry for her and had left a picnic basket with a few things for her supper. Of course, the fact that the "few things" consisted of a platter of fried chicken and a sweet potato pie just proved how much she really was needed here. But in her present mellow mood, she decided to splurge and enjoy them anyway. Monday she'd get back on the wagon and start her campaign to tone up Silver Creek.

The VFW hall was decked out with red-and-white crepe paper streamers, and a large hand-lettered sign announced Welcome Miss Lindsey! Susannah noted as she pulled into the parking lot. Silver Creek was certainly going all out on her behalf, and she was touched.

Was she overdressed? she wondered as she stepped out of the car and adjusted the collar on her simple turquoise shirtwaist. She'd wanted to look well-groomed and professional and yet still fit in with what she expected was a very casual life-style in town. Her concerns were allayed as she reached the building and the women she spotted entering it. Apparently, anything from Bermuda shorts to sundresses was acceptable.

The large double front doors swung open before Susannah had a chance to reach for them. A dozen or so people, including Nora Mae and Dwayne Rollins, surged out to meet her. The mayor and his wife had stopped in yesterday evening to see if she was "settlin' in all right."

Amidst a flurry of hellos and handshakes, Susannah was swept inside. Then the beaming mayor and his wife escorted her around the room and presented her to various groups. She could imagine that a prize-winning heifer at the county fair might get similar treatment.

"And this is Charlie and Donna Nevins. Charlie's an accountant, and Donna runs our preschool. Donna's also on the town council, and she was one of your biggest advocates," Nora Mae explained as they came to a stop.

"I'm delighted to meet you," Susannah murmured.

"If you're not careful, Susannah's going to put you on a diet, Charlie," Donna teased as he downed a handful of cheese puffs from a basket that was being passed around.

"Shoot, he's already on a diet—a seafood diet," the mayor cut in.

The newcomer looked in puzzlement at the cheese puffs. "Seafood?"

"Whenever Charlie sees food, he eats it!" the mayor said, slapping his thigh and hooting.

Susannah found herself laughing as heartily as the rest of the group at the silly joke. Then they resumed chatting. The Nevinses seemed very likeable, and Susannah realized she was enjoying the conversation.

In the middle of the interchange, the feeling of being watched made her glance up. Her gaze collided with that of a tall, startlingly attractive man who was leaning nonchalantly against one of the wooden columns supporting the roof. His hair had the casual windblown look that men she knew achieved with mousse and a blow dryer. She suspected that he came by the style more naturally—probably in some sort of outdoor occupation. In a purely professional way, of course, she was admiring the way the green knit shirt stretched across his broad shoulders, when she realized Donna was waiting for the answer to a question.

"Sorry. What did you say?"

Making a determined effort, she turned her attention back to the conversation. Then, after a few minutes, her self-appointed guides insisted she needed to keep moving.

All the introductions made her head swim. Perhaps that was why it took her a moment to find her voice when Nora Mae Rollins led her up to the only person in the room she hadn't yet met.

"And this is another of our town's leading citizens," the mayor's wife chirped. "Susannah Lindsey, Brett Tanner, president of the Chamber of Commerce."

He looked as if he'd be more at home at the helm of a windjammer than running a business, Susannah thought. Across the room his rakish good looks had appealed to her. Now she couldn't suppress a little shiver as his vivid blue eyes focused on her face. He certainly had sex appeal to burn. But she suspected that her response was as much to the challenge that she read on his virile features as to anything else.

"Brett owns the best marina on the Carolina coast," Nora Mae was saying.

That explained the sun-bleached hair, enviable tan and rock-hard muscles, Susannah mused. "Nice to meet you," she offered in what she hoped was a neutral tone.

"You, too," he drawled noncommittally.

"Brett is also on the town council," Nora Mae explained as the conversation lagged.

"Good. Then I take it you're already interested in our program of fitness and exercise." Susannah tried to make small talk.

"Not really. I get all I need on the job." The denial was pleasant, and so was the smile, but Susannah sensed an underlying coolness.

"Of course, every now and then I exercise my right to go fishing—and I do coach the Little League baseball team," he continued.

"I doubt that fishing ranks as one of the top hundred aerobic activities. But, then again, I've never done it."

"Well, I'd have to say you don't look like the fishing type."

She wasn't sure what to make of that, but Brett Tanner didn't give her time to respond.

"I want to have a word with my son before the dinner starts." With that he excused himself.

Susannah watched as he threaded his way across the room. Given his youthful looks, she'd pictured him leaning down to talk to a grade-schooler. Instead he stopped before a towheaded boy who came well up to his shoulders. Even from this distance she could see the family resemblance. When the senior Tanner moved on, her eyes couldn't help following until his tall, athletic body disappeared into the crowd, a fact that her hostess quickly noticed.

"Brett's Silver Creek's most eligible bachelor," Nora Mae put in. "He was a big executive up in Philadelphia for a while. But he moved back home with his son when his wife died about four years ago."

Susannah nodded as she digested that information, along with its implications. In just a day and a half she'd discovered that Silver Creek was a lot friendlier than Atlanta, where she didn't know most of the people in her condominium complex. But there was another side to the coin, as well. In this small town, apparently everyone knew everyone else—and their business as well. And she could bet that juicy gossip would travel faster than on the national news wire service.

"Fine-looking young man, isn't he?" the older woman continued. "A charmer, too."

Was she talking about the father or the son? Susannah wondered. She murmured a noncommittal "Umm-hmm." She'd have to agree the senior Tanner was certainly fine-looking. She'd even go as far as devastating. But charming?

There was no time to discuss Brett's qualities further, however, because her hostess was anxious to have Susannah officially begin the supper. A sturdy paper plate and plastic utensils were thrust into her hand, and she was guided to the long tables crowded with dozens of casseroles and bowls.

"I hardly know where to begin," Susannah said with a sigh. The section directly in front of her contained the salads—with a heavy emphasis on potatoes, macaroni and sweet-gelatin molds. The only leafy greens she could see were smothered in thick, creamy dressing.

"Try that banana-pecan salad," the grandmotherly woman behind her encouraged. "The recipe's been my family's favorite for years. And you've got to taste Nora Mae's deviled eggs; Dwayne can eat 'em a dozen at a time."

Susannah smiled weakly and put a dab of the salad on her plate. The women in Silver Creek had obviously gone to a lot of trouble to impress her, but the food they'd prepared was far richer than she could advocate for everyday consumption. If they ate like this all the time, nutrition education was one area she'd have to see to right away.

There were more pies and cakes than main dishes or salads. The prospect of tasting them all and then having to work off the calories the next day was daunting.

"I think I'll just start with dinner and go back for dessert later," she explained.

"I plan to do that myself. Feel free to go back for as much as you want," Nora Mae reassured.

Balancing her plate and a cup of presweetened iced tea, Susannah followed her hostess to the head table.

"Since you're the guest of honor, we want you to sit here," the older woman said, gesturing.

Susannah took a seat and began chatting about plans for the program with the couple across the table. The places around her quickly filled with the town's dignitaries, and soon only the seat to her right remained unclaimed. She turned at the scraping noise to find the empty chair being pulled back. "I guess I have the honor of sitting next to our celebrity guest," Brett observed as he eased his tall frame into the cramped space.

Susannah gave him a measured look. If he was thrilled with the prospect, he was hiding it well. "It appears so," she agreed. Her stomach did a quick flip-flop of anticipation and dread. It was disconcerting to be in such close quarters with the man she'd found most attractive and at the same time the least hospitable. She tried to scoot over to give him more room, but there was nowhere to go.

"Two dinner plates?" She couldn't help commenting as he set the pair of dishes in front of him.

"Well, I didn't want to hurt any of the ladies' feelings," he drawled. "Besides, I'm not on a diet."

"You do look in good shape. But there are other reasons for a healthy diet besides losing weight."

Brett's bronze-tinged brows momentarily arched as he considered how to respond. Any man who wasn't stone was bound to respond to Susannah Lindsey. She might be dressed in a simple shirtwaist this evening, but he couldn't stop himself from picturing the way she'd looked in that leotard on the exercise tape. Now that he was sitting with his leg inches from hers, it was hard to be indifferent to her well-toned body, not to mention those sultry brown eyes and soft, inviting lips. It took an effort to remind himself that the fancy packaging hid an opportunist who had jumped at the chance to sell Silver Creek something it didn't need.

Beauty really was only skin deep, he mused. His wife certainly hadn't been beautiful. But she'd been everything he wanted in a woman, which was why he hadn't gotten serious about anyone else.

He was annoyed to realize that he was tempted by the attractive veneer of the woman sitting next to him, and he gave in to the sudden uncharacteristic impulse to be rude. "My observation is that most folks really don't need to go on a diet," he said conversationally, his voice pitched so that no one on either side of them could hear. "Of course, there's a whole industry built on convincing them that they do."

Susannah's fork stopped in midair. She set it down very carefully so she wouldn't accidentally drop the pecan-coated banana slice into her lap—or intentionally into his. Though the man had delivered the line casually, she knew it was intended as a thinly veiled insult. She'd already sensed that he wasn't one of her biggest fans in town, but she'd had no idea he was actually hostile.

"I see you have a strong opinion on the subject. Should I try to confuse you with a few facts, or is your mind already made up, Mr. Tanner?"

"Oh, I can be reasonable when I want to," Brett allowed, ignoring her quick return jab. He'd probably been too blunt, but she might as well know where he stood. "By the way, call me Brett; I'm sure I'd like that better than what you're considering."

"I'm sure you would," Susannah agreed coolly. His behavior had certainly thrown her off balance. On the one hand, he was good-humoredly acknowledging that he knew he'd provoked her, yet he was also making it clear he had no intention of apologizing or taking his challenging remark back.

"I gather you feel that all efforts to promote fitness and good health are a waste of time and motivated by greed," she commented sweetly.

"Well, let's just say that I'm suspicious. It seems as though someone's always hyping a crazy new exercise program, like hanging upside down from a hook on the ceiling. Or some new diet book or videotape," he continued, "that promises you can lose twenty inches and fifteen pounds in four days or lower your cholesterol by drinking radish juice. If all this stuff worked as advertised, then we wouldn't be seeing a new scam coming down the pike every week."

Susannah kept her voice level. "It's perfectly true there are frauds in the health industry, as there are in every other kind of business. But just because a few 'doctors' practice with a mail-order degree doesn't mean we should give up modern medicine for herbs and leeches. It's the same in the nutrition and physical-fitness fields. There's a lot of legitimate work being done that can help people live longer, healthier lives."

"I'm sure you've got a stack of statistics to back you up," he said, picking up a peanut-butter-stuffed celery stalk and waving it for emphasis. "But then, that's what you get paid for, isn't it? Besides, too many facts and figures can cause indigestion." He shrugged and bit into the celery stick with a loud crunch to signal the discussion was closed.

Susannah's brown eyes flashed with indignation, and she cast a quick glance at the group around them. Everyone else was either deep in conversation or enjoying the food. So she counted to ten and strove to keep the acrimonious exchange between herself and Brett.

"It's obvious you aren't really interested in talking about this, so let's be frank, Mr. Tanner. I was hired to help Silver Creek get into shape, and I fully intend to do my job." She drew in an irritated breath. "From what I've seen so far, the whole community—with one exception—seems enthusiastic about the project. I want you to know your support would be welcome, but it certainly isn't essential."

"Then we understand each other." He turned back to his meal.

Susannah clenched her teeth and resisted the urge to argue further. She was usually pretty even-tempered. But ten minutes in the company of this man had raised her blood pressure and set her nerves on edge. Somehow, the fact that he was attractive and she had responded to him on that physical level irritated her even more. She'd had friendlier encounters with yellow jackets.

For a few minutes Susannah pretended to concentrate on her own plate. Then she pointedly leaned away from Brett and struck up a conversation with the couple across the table.

To her annoyance, even as she chatted about her job with Healthways, she was aware of the man sitting beside her. He was sharing a fishing story with the grandfatherly type on his left and seemed to have quickly recovered his sense of humor.

Her eavesdropping was interrupted by Mayor Rollins. "Testing, one, two, three. Can y'all hear me out there?" he asked, tapping the mike that had been set up at the front of the room. There were scattered affirmative hoots and whistles. "Calvin Boyd and the Rockabillies are here the rest of the evening to provide some dancing music for us," he announced. "And I'd like our special guest, Miss Lindsey, to lead off the first number. Brett, will you do the honors?"

Susannah watched as, without a word, Brett rose and helped her to her feet. Then with a flourish, he offered his arm and escorted her to the middle of the room. She was sure that no one could tell how detestable the idea of being together was to both of them. Unless, of course, they got a close-up of her partner's face. Beneath that polite smile his expression held about as much enthusiasm as a condemned prisoner's in front of a firing squad.

"Shall we dance?" he asked as he took her in his arms.

For the first few beats he held her stiffly. Then the music seemed to work a transformation. It was a soft country-rock number that she'd never thought of dancing to before. The lyrics were about a man and woman whose "daytime fightin' turned to nighttime lovin'."

The fingers at her waist drew her closer. The hand that had simply been a resting place for hers enfolded her fingers and held them against his chest.

The unaccountably possessive gesture made her aware of Brett in a way that she sensed was dangerous. But she couldn't stop herself from enjoying the feeling of warmth that enveloped her from being in his arms. He smelled of sea breezes and sunshine and an indefinable, unique scent. She'd seen that his muscles were well-conditioned, so she hadn't been prepared for the sensation of being gently encircled by tempered steel.

Other dancers had joined them on the floor. But they were only shadows flickering at the edges of her awareness. Susannah made an effort to break the spell. She and Brett were virtual strangers, and they didn't even like each other.

The music stopped, and she tried to back away, but the steel she'd sensed beneath the surface of his corded arms suddenly locked her into place.

She expected him to say something, but he didn't speak. When the next song started, he simply pulled her closer. She could either follow his lead or make a scene. Under the circumstances, she had no real option but to go along with him. At least, that was what she rationalized as her softness molded itself to his hard strength.

Chapter Two

Usually Susannah awoke to the sound of traffic rushing past her condo, not a chorus of warblers in the trees outside her window.

At first she was disoriented. Then she remembered. Silver Creek. The program she'd come to set up. And the town supper the night before to welcome her. Everybody had been so glad to meet her—except Brett Tanner.

He'd been rude and disagreeable. Then why had she melted like butter on hot toast when he'd taken her in his arms and whirled her around the dance floor? The memory made her cheeks burn.

But it hadn't been all one-sided, she reminded herself. She'd known he was responding to her just the way she'd responded to him. What she didn't understand was how the two of them could be physically attracted when they couldn't even carry on a civil conversation.

What had Nora Mae called him? "Silver Creek's most eligible bachelor." Maybe he thought he could make time with her because she was a fast city lady.

Well, he was dead wrong. And she was going to make sure he understood that she was immune to his charms—particularly in light of the way he'd made it clear he didn't think much of her profession.

Susannah glanced at the clock on the nightstand. It was only eight-thirty. She had an hour and a half before the meeting with the town's community leaders. So she threw on a robe over her batiste gown and made herself a cup of strawberry-herb tea and two slices of whole-wheat toast. In the refrigerator was a jar of Nora Mae's homemade peach preserves. A tiny spoonful wouldn't hurt. Particularly if she didn't use butter, too.

She carried her breakfast out to the screened porch at the back of the house and sat down to go over the notes for her presentation. But the country setting was so novel that she finally put the papers down and watched a couple of squirrels chase each other from the branches of a maple to an oak. It was amazing how they could leap through the air like that, she thought, and land without falling to the ground.

Then she smiled. It had been a long time since she'd sat still long enough to make that kind of observation. Usually she left for work early in the morning and didn't get home until after dark. During the day, she was so busy that she rushed from the TV studio, where she taped her shows, to the health club, where she taught her classes, and never had time to look around.

A few minutes later she picked up her notes again and settled down to work. One reason she could come to Silver Creek for a fraction of her usual fee was that she'd designed this kind of total fitness program before. Two years ago she'd put together a package for the Davis Corporation, one of Atlanta's largest computer companies. Her health program had been well received by the employees and management and had been praised as one of the best in the country.

She'd promised herself she was going to give Silver Creek a first-rate program, too. She had to make a good presentation and be able to answer questions afterward. Knowing that her audience's first impression of the way she handled herself was important to how well her suggestions went over, she chose to dress conservatively in a navy-blue spring suit and a blue-and-white print blouse.

When she arrived at city hall, Mayor Rollins was just finishing arranging several rows of wooden folding chairs in the assembly room. Then he went out to get a couple of large electric fans.

"This place sure heats up like a furnace in the warm weather," he apologized. "By next week we ought to have the air-conditioning fixed. Burt's going to get right to it after he finishes wiring the new addition to his house."

Members of the business community began to drift in. Susannah had met most of them the night before. By five of ten, the rows of chairs were almost full.

It annoyed her to realize she kept looking up to see if Brett had decided to honor her with his presence. She wasn't sure whether she wanted to see him or not. But when he hadn't arrived by ten after the hour, she told herself she was glad.

"You know, after that wonderful spread last night, I'm going to have to hide out from all the good cooks in town or else I won't be able to touch my toes," Susannah began.

After the appreciative laughter, she went on to say that the town's interest in home cooking was really a plus.

"The most nutritious meals are the ones made from scratch," she added. "You just have to learn how to maximize the taste and minimize the calories."

"I was afraid you were going to make us eat health-food glop that tastes like sawdust," someone in the audience confessed.

There was nervous laughter from the audience.

"How do crab-stuffed flounder or tarragon chicken sound?" Susannah countered.

"Mighty fine," the mayor assured her.

As she outlined more of her program, Susannah was glad to note that the businessmen and -women were a receptive audience.

"I'm pleased to be working with all of you," she went on. "Together, I think we can really make your health-and-nutrition program a big success with everyone in the community."

She'd just begun talking about details of the program when the door at the back of the room eased open and Brett sauntered in.

Most of the people were well dressed; he was wearing a white T-shirt and faded jeans with a hole in one knee.

There were no chairs left in the last row. Instead of coming up to the front of the room, he propped his lean hips against the wall and crossed his arms.

His eyes met Susannah's, and for a moment she couldn't for the life of her think what she had intended to say next. As she looked down at her notes, trying to find her place, the silence seemed to stretch forever. But she suspected it only seemed like a moment to the audience before she began to speak again.

To her own ears, the rest of the presentation didn't sound quite as smooth as it had at the beginning. But she covered everything she intended to—from a healthy cooking contest to exercise options for all ages.

"If you're agreeable, I'd like to have some of the programs started by next week," she concluded. "And I'll be getting the word out through the local paper."

"I'll be glad to make announcements, too," Dave Caldwell from the local radio station put in.

When Susannah finished, she drew a hearty round of applause from everyone except Brett, who kept his arms crossed. There was an unreadable expression on his tanned face. Susannah imagined that he'd rather be out fishing. Why had he bothered to come?

"Well, it looks as if everybody's rarin' to get started," the mayor enthused after she answered half a dozen questions.

"There are a lot of resources in Silver Creek," Donna added. "But I'm thinking you're going to need someone with a good handle on the town to advise you."

In the back of the room, Brett had straightened and started to inch silently toward the door. Susannah was the only one who could see him. No one else realized he'd come in late.

"Someone who knows how to get things done," Bonnie seconded the observation.

"Someone who has a little slack time now before the tourist season starts," Dwayne mused.

Was it Susannah's imagination, or had these three people already discussed this issue? Was this a setup?

Before she could speculate further, Donna came in right on cue. "I know just the person," she announced. "Brett Tanner. And he's not here, so he can't object."

The man in question was already most of the way out the door. Susannah had never seen anyone reenter a room so fast.

"Yes, he is," Brett's baritone voice rang out from the back of the hall.

All heads swiveled in his direction.

"Glad you could make it, boy," the mayor drawled.

"I like the common courtesy of being consulted before I'm elected to any new position."

"Oh, that's a hoot. Remember the time I had a real bad head cold and came back to find you had appointed me chairwoman of the town square clean-up committee?" Bonnie reminded him.

Under his tan, Brett had the grace to flush.

Everyone in the hall laughed.

"That's one of the ways we get people to meetings," Dwayne confided to Susannah in a conspiratorial whisper.

Brett strolled slowly up to the front of the room, looking directly at Susannah as he approached her.

She didn't flinch from the challenge in his sea-blue eyes.

"If Ms. Lindsey's agreeable to the arrangement, so am I."

Susannah knew what she wanted to say, but she simply didn't dare insult one of the town business leaders in front of his peers. "I'd be delighted to have Mr. Tanner's help," she heard herself agreeing sweetly.

"Then it's settled," Dwayne announced, putting the official seal of approval on the arrangement.

People began to get up. Some stood talking in little groups. Others came up to have a private word with

Susannah. Finally she and Brett were left alone at the front of the hall.

He walked over and shut off the electric fans.

Susannah hadn't realized how comforting their hum had been. To fill the sudden quiet in the room, she shuffled her notes together.

Brett seemed content to let the silence lengthen. And she was darned if she was going to give him the satisfaction of being the first one to say something. She studied the aggressive set of his strong jaw. It didn't quite go with the easy way he was lounging against the mantelpiece.

There were a lot of things she didn't understand about Brett, Susannah admitted to herself. He appeared to be as laid-back as everyone else in Silver Creek, but somehow she knew instinctively that he was a man who was used to having people go along with his ideas.

Susannah was aware that while she was studying him, he was making his own assessment of her. Was he remembering the way she'd swayed against him when they'd danced last night? She was certainly thinking about it. Was that why the room felt warm? Or was it just because the fans were off?

Unconsciously her eyes traveled down his well-muscled form. Searching for a safe place to focus, they found the rip in the knee of his jeans. He needed someone to patch it for him, she mused, before bringing herself up short.

"Well?" he finally drawled.

The best way to deal with this man was to bring the issue right out into the open. "I had the distinct impression you were about to opt out. What made you change your mind?" she challenged.

"I figured it gave me the chance to make sure you don't get into any trouble around here."

"Trouble? Why, Mr. Tanner, what did you have in mind?"

He acknowledged the parry with a grin. "Nothing yet. But I'm working on it."

She chose not to rise to the bait. "Do you have any real intention of helping me?"

"What do you think?" he shot back.

"I think you're not about to give me a straight answer."

He threw back his head and laughed. "You city girls are pretty smart."

"And you country boys aren't as dumb as you act."

"Why, thank you, Ms. Lindsey." With that he turned and walked out of the room.

After that barbed exchange, Susannah didn't really expect any help from Brett. The most she could hope for was that he'd stay out of her way so she could get her job done.

That afternoon Susannah asked Mayor Rollins for a room in the city hall that she could use as a base of operations.

He scratched his bald head and thought for a moment. "Afraid there aren't any vacant offices. But we can probably squeeze you into the room where Sheriff Lovejoy gives drivers tests once a week, if that'll do."

When Susannah looked a bit doubtful, he added, "You could schedule an exercise class on Tuesdays and miss all those nervous teenagers who are sweating out their first exam."

He led her down to an office at the end of the hall. The room was sparsely furnished with an old wooden desk and a row of folding chairs. For a moment, Susannah thought about her spacious, carpeted office back at Healthways. Then she noticed the lovely view of the town square outside the window.

"This will do fine," she assured him.

When the mayor left, Susannah settled into her new office. After the morning's enthusiastic response from the business community, she was anxious to follow up on the offers of support as well as pursue others. She found the Chamber of Commerce directory and the yellow pages in the bottom drawer of her desk and started making phone calls. She set up appointments over the next two days with the grocery-store manager, the newspaper editor, the radio-station owner and the supervisor of the Quick Print Shop.

All of them were very responsive. After only a couple of meetings, Susannah realized that it was easy to appeal to the merchants' sense of community spirit.

Quick Print offered to do her menus and class schedules for free—if she'd give them a line at the bottom stating that they'd donated their services. That was a good thing because she really didn't have much of a budget.

Paul Demotto at Eddy's Market agreed to run specials on ingredients she'd be using in her weekly menus. He was excited at the prospect of distributing the menus.

"You're not going to get people to change their cooking habits unless you tell 'em how," he pointed out. Then a light bulb seemed to go on over his head. "You could even do cooking demonstrations right here at the store."

"I hadn't thought of that," Susannah admitted. "But it's a good idea." She made a note in the little spiral-bound book she kept in her purse.

At the radio station, WSIL, Dave Caldwell greeted her enthusiastically. "I've saved a spot for you on our weekly call-in program," he said.

"Would it be all right if I waited to start until the week after next?" Susannah asked.

Dave's brow furrowed. "Sure. I guess we can fill in this week with Aunt Dotty. She's been wanting to tell Silver Creek about her trip to Alaska. Too bad she can't show her slides on the radio."

All in all, Susannah was feeling pretty positive by the time she went back to the grocery store to do her own shopping. It gave her a sense of satisfaction to assure herself that she'd done it all without any help from Brett.

It was late, and Eddy's Market was almost empty. In the produce department, she selected two boxes of luscious-looking local strawberries and some tender green asparagus along with a large supply of salad ingredients.

But even though she was shopping for herself, her mind was on the first batch of recipes she'd be presenting to the community.

Asparagus vinaigrette—light on the oil.

Strawberries Romanoff—made with low-fat ricotta instead of sour cream.

All she needed was a main dish, with either chicken or fish.

Susannah had just finished at the dairy case and turned the corner when she spotted Brett at the end of the aisle. He was wearing a slightly wrinkled cotton shirt and a pair of faded jeans slung low on his hips.

Well, speak of the devil, she thought.

Susannah wasn't all that surprised to see that he was loading his cart with bags of sour-cream potato chips.

Next he moved on to the soft drinks and began picking up cartons of soda.

He hadn't seen her. And she couldn't resist following discreetly behind him to see what other dreadful stuff he routinely purchased.

As if on cue, he pushed his cart to the bakery section and began loading up on cupcakes as if he suspected there was going to be a shortage next week.

No wonder he'd been so hostile, Susannah mused. The man was obviously a junk-food addict.

At that moment he turned and spotted her. She knew by his wry expression that he had caught the disapproving look on her face. Or maybe he had the grace to be embarrassed.

"Why, if it isn't Miss Lite-and-Lively."

Susannah fought back a grin. Trust him to defend himself with humor.

He peered into her cart. "Yum! Is all of that for you—or your pet hamster?"

Susannah knew she should just shrug and walk on. But she made the mistake of sweeping her eyes over his cart again.

His gaze followed hers.

"Is that the kind of food you bring home to a growing boy?"

"Sometimes."

"Well, let me tell you that bad eating habits learned in childhood haunt an adult through his entire life."

"Do tell." The words were light. But the teasing expression on his face had been replaced with something more defensive.

Susannah was too wound up to quit now. "There's enough saturated fat and cholesterol in that cart to kill twenty laboratory rats."

Instead of answering, he shrugged.

They were standing there staring at each other when a boyish shout rang out from the end of the aisle. "Dad, the ice-cream cake for my birthday party is gonna melt if you don't hurry up."

Before Brett could answer, his son had already made his way to the cart and looked in. "Aw, Dad, you don't even have the pizza stuff yet."

Brett put a hand on his son's shoulder. "Let's not forget our manners, young man."

"Oh, yeah, sorry."

"Susannah Lindsey, this is my son, Billy," Brett continued. "Billy, this is Miss Lindsey."

"Pleased to meet you," they both responded.

Brett turned back to his son. "Why don't you pick up the cheese and the crusts? I'll get the tomato sauce."

"Okay, Dad." Billy charged off toward the dairy section.

Susannah eyed Brett. "Speaking of manners, you could have told me you were getting ready for a special occasion, instead of letting me make a fool of myself."

He grinned. "You're right cute when you're up on your soapbox."

She flushed.

"You know how kids are about birthday parties. I'd better finish up."

Susannah nodded, remembering how it had been when she was a girl. Her—and her brother's—parties had always been high points of the year. It was just one of the ways her parents had shown their children that they loved them very much.

As she watched Brett push his cart around the corner, she wished she hadn't been so quick to make judgments. From that brief exchange with his son, she could sense that same kind of closeness that had made her own childhood warm and secure.

The next morning Mayor Rollins paused in the doorway of Susannah's office. "From what I hear around town, it seems like you've been busy as a mother hen with a brood of chicks." The mayor came in and propped his ample hip against the edge of her desk.

"Have the local businessmen been giving you reports?" Susannah asked.

"Nothing formal. But you can't do anything in this town without word gettin' around."

Susannah nodded. She'd only been in Silver Creek six days, but every day in the community made her realize how much different life was here than back in Atlanta. At home she wore a suit to work when she wasn't teaching an exercise class. Down here her mint-green sundress and sandals were just right. But because of the heat and her professional image, she did sweep her thick hair up into a French twist that kept it off her neck.

"Anything else you need?" Dwayne asked.

"There is one thing. I still don't have a good place to hold my exercise classes."

"Hmm. Didn't you and our liaison person get around to discussing that at Eddy's Market last night?"

Susannah blinked. The grocery store had been virtually deserted. She looked at her watch. It was nine a.m.—only twelve hours since she and Brett had encountered each other at the food store—and they were already an item on the local gossip circuit.

"No, we didn't get around to that," Susannah murmured.

"Well, don't fret about it. He's in the building this morning, and I asked him to stop by."

"How nice."

"Glad you're looking forward to it." The comment had come from the doorway.

Susannah looked up to see Brett standing there. She noted that he was a bit more dressed up than he had been the last two times she'd seen him. His cream-colored, short-sleeve shirt was crisp. Had he ironed it himself? she wondered. He'd also exchanged his faded jeans for a pair of navy cotton twill slacks.

The man looked good. Susannah followed his progress as he crossed the room and took one of the folding chairs provided for driver's-license applicants.

Dwayne stood up. "Miss Lindsey says she needs a place to hold her exercise classes. You goin' to take her around?"

"If she wants me to." Brett gave her a noncommittal look. His posture remained relaxed as he stretched out his long legs.

Susannah didn't know what Dwayne had heard about last night's encounter at Eddy's Market. But she certainly didn't want to provide any more grist for the town gossip mill. "Whenever you have time," she said in a businesslike voice.

"No time like the present."

"Well, I'll leave you kids to get on with it," Dwayne said. His rotund body paused in the doorway. "I sure am looking forward to those exercise classes," he drawled.

"You're going to participate?" Susannah couldn't quite hide the surprise in her voice.

He shook his head. "Heck, no! I'm just going to observe." He winked at Brett, and the two men grinned at each other.

When the mayor had left the room, Susannah looked inquiringly at Brett lounging in the corner. "What was that all about?"

"I think it started with that tape of Toning Your Tummy and Other Parts. How do you think the ladies sold your program to the guys on the town council, anyway?"

Susannah flushed. She hadn't thought about it in quite those terms. "Well, whatever. I need a hall big enough to hold the classes. Are you serious about showing me some suitable locations?"

"Yes, ma'am."

Susannah collected her purse from a desk drawer, and they both went out into the parking lot. She followed Brett to a somewhat-battered silver pickup truck. He was probably waiting to see if she'd object. Well, it wasn't her usual mode of transportation, but she didn't comment as he held open the door. Inside, the vehicle was a lot more plush than she expected, judging from the outside. The upholstery was comfortable, and there was an expensive-looking cassette deck and radio system.

Brett offered her a selection of cassettes. She was surprised he liked some of the same music that she did. Whitney Houston. Alabama. And some Broadway musicals.

She picked *Les Misérables*, which she'd seen on a business trip to New York.

"That's one of my favorite shows," Brett said.

"You saw it?" She couldn't hide the surprise in her voice.

He nodded casually. "Sometimes we country boys make it to the big city. I took Billy on a trip to New York a couple of summers ago."

"I saw it there, too," was the only response she could think of at the moment.

They both listened to the music as Brett headed down Main Street. It was a beautiful day. The sun was shining. The sky was clear blue. And every yard was bright with flowers.

"I've already found out I can't use the VFW hall because of the day-care center they run there during the week," Susannah said.

"Yeah, I know. I was thinking about a couple of other places."

A few moments later he pulled into the parking lot beside the colonial-style red brick church she'd noticed when she first drove into town.

The entrance was flanked with beds of red and white geraniums. Susannah stopped for a moment to admire them.

Brett took her arm to usher her inside. "This place has a big basement. And they don't use it for anything much," he said.

There was an undertone in his voice that made Susannah wonder what he was up to. Given his attitude about her project, she didn't quite trust the helpful act he was putting on now.

To Susannah's surprise, the building wasn't locked. "You mean we can just walk in?" she whispered, her voice automatically taking on a hushed tone as they crossed the threshold.

"Silver Creek isn't exactly the crime capital of the U.S.," he threw over his shoulder affably.

A stairway at the side of the lobby led down into the basement. Although Brett flipped on a light switch, there wasn't much illumination. A musty odor rose up toward Susannah as she followed Brett down toward a dark hallway.

The basement presented a sharp contrast to the marble floors, polished wood and white, fluted columns upstairs. Susannah shivered in her light sundress and wrapped her arms around her shoulders. She would have liked to climb back up the stairs and into the warmth of the spring day again. But she didn't want Brett to be able to say that she'd dismissed the place without even checking it out.

There were several doors off the hall.

"It's the last one on the right," Brett told her. In the underground hall, his voice had taken on a hollow timbre.

Susannah made herself march resolutely up to the door and throw it open. The room was even worse than she'd imagined. The strong smell of mildew made her nose wrinkle. Cobwebs hung from the ceiling like decorations in a haunted house. The only illumination was provided by two single, bare bulbs.

It wouldn't be easy getting the place cleaned up. Susannah took a cautious step forward and almost tripped on the uneven cement floor. She was about to make a disparaging comment when a rustling sound in the corner made her freeze. In the next moment, a furry shape scurried right across her open-toed sandal. A mouse!

Susannah had never wanted to scream more in her life. Or to grab for a man's reassuringly broad shoulders—Brett's. But she knew he was standing right behind her waiting to see if she'd go to pieces. Probably he'd dragged her down here to enjoy her reaction.

Before she turned to face him in the dim light, she composed her features. "I don't think this place is going to work out—for a number of reasons I'm sure you can appreciate,'' she said, surprised at how steady her voice sounded.

His arms were crossed in that characteristic gesture that Susannah had come to associate with him.

''Don't picture yourself cleaning out cobwebs?''

She ignored his condescending tone. ''Oh, I could handle that. But the lighting is pretty bad. And if we tried to do aerobics on this floor, Doc Crowley would be treating a room full of sprained ankles.''

''I see.''

''Are you really trying to help me, or are we just playing games?''

He regarded her steadily for a moment, as if considering the validity of her question. ''Extra light's no problem. But I hadn't thought about the floor.''

She looked meaningfully around the subterranean chamber. ''Because you don't know an exercise room from a hole in the ground!''

Chapter Three

He threw back his head and laughed. "All right, Miss Lindsey. There is another hall I can show you."

Susannah marched out of the musty room. "The next place better be good," she muttered under her breath as they climbed back up the stairs.

For the first part of the ride to the other possible exercise room, there was an awkward silence between them.

"When I came back to Silver Creek four years ago, the economy was stagnating," Brett finally remarked as they drove up Main Street into the business district. It was like those in a lot of Southern towns—with small stores lined up along either side of the street. Many of them had been recently painted and spruced up.

"It looks pretty prosperous now."

"Umm-hmm. But four years ago I was worried about whether a place this size could support a profitable marina," Brett continued.

Susannah tucked a wayward strand of hair back into the French twist at the back of her neck. He'd managed to pique her interest. "You were?"

She could feel Brett's gaze on her as she pulled out a hairpin and replaced it. In the close confines of the truck cab, the casual gesture suddenly seemed intimate.

Brett appeared to have lost his train of thought. "Yes, well," he started up again, "after doing an informal market analysis, I advised the town council and the Chamber of Commerce to go out after the tourist trade."

He pulled into a parking space in front of a large barnlike building at the eastern end of the business district. "The old livery stable," Brett explained as he climbed out of the truck and put a coin in the meter.

Susannah noted that a dime was going to give him an hour's worth of parking. Where she came from, it would have been more like a quarter for fifteen minutes.

She looked with appreciation at the building. Obviously a lot of care had been taken with the restoration. The siding had been painted a colonial gray with white trim. There were double-wide wooden doors with brass trim. A large octagonal window had been built into the second-story gable.

"Four years ago, they were planning to tear this thing down. Instead, we decided to turn it into a craft-and-produce market on the weekends. The idea worked out pretty well all around." Brett threw open the door and ushered Susannah inside.

She found herself in a large, bright room. Paneling covered the walls, and wooden booths had been built side to side, forming several aisles.

"You could only use this place Monday through Thursday," Brett said. "Which could be pretty inconvenient. That's why I didn't bring you here first."

The setting had an appealing country charm. The room was airy. The floor looked suitable. And the lighting was good. But what about the booths? They appeared to be pretty permanent.

Susannah turned to Brett. "How would I move the booths?"

"You can't. But there's an empty loft above this room." Brett led her up a wooden stairway to the second level. Under a high-bowed roof with handsome exposed beams and several skylights was a space that would make a wonderful exercise room.

"What do you think?"

"It's perfect," Susannah responded. "Except for the heat."

"There's an air-conditioning system. It's just not on now."

"I assume there are rest rooms downstairs."

"Right."

"Do you think we can get the owner to donate the space?"

"I have some pull with the owner."

"Who is it?"

He grinned. "Me. The town couldn't afford to buy the property and take on the renovation. So I financed the project through the investment firm I used to work for."

The explanation reinforced Susannah's impression that Brett was a complex man. He gave the appearance of being an easygoing good old boy. But underneath he was not only a savvy businessman but also a community benefactor.

"You can have the space during the week," Brett continued.

She gave him a direct look. "Ever since I got here you've made no secret of your opposition to my program. Why the sudden about-face?"

The very smallest hint of a smile flickered at the corners of his lips. "I learned some lessons in the corporate boardroom that are just as applicable in Silver Creek as they were in Philadelphia."

"I've got to hear this."

"You can oppose a project all the way up to the final decision to implement it. Then you have to fall in line and support the corporate policy."

"I got the distinct feeling you were still opposing the project after I arrived in Silver Creek," Susannah pointed out.

"Umm-hmm," he admitted. "That's because I still didn't know how serious you were."

"Oh, I'm very serious."

"I know. And since you are, I want to make sure Silver Creek is getting good value for its investment."

She planted her hands firmly on her hips. "For your information, I'm working at far less than my usual fee."

"Well then, you must be getting something besides money out of this. What?"

"The satisfaction of helping people who really need it," Susannah shot back.

"Is that all?"

Susannah turned away and pretended to give the loft a closer inspection. There *was* more to her coming to town. She had wanted to escape from the hectic pace of her life, at least for a little while. But she wasn't about to get into a life-style discussion with Brett.

Yet their frank exchange had cleared the air—up to a certain point.

"If it would make you feel better about using my facility, you could do a favor for me," Brett suggested.

Susannah nodded. That was something she had learned about the corporate world. When someone went out of their way for you, it was expected that they would ask something in return. "Such as?"

"I could use your help with a project that's turning out to be a bit more of a problem than I anticipated." There was a slight note of chagrin in his voice.

Susannah looked at him, warily wishing she knew how to gauge him. "What's that?" she inquired cautiously.

He shifted his weight to his right leg. "Surviving Billy's birthday party tonight." His voice lowered to the tone of an old-time radio announcer. "The Invasion of the Twelve-Year-Olds."

Susannah laughed.

"My son talked me into letting him have twelve friends over because it's his twelfth birthday. But there's only so much that a grown man can do by himself."

Susannah remembered her brother's parties. "I'm not sure I'd be much help," she ventured.

"Oh, you'd be a lot of help. In the first place, you're a woman, which automatically limits the kind of stunts they're going to pull. In the second place, you're an honored guest of the town, which might make them be on their best behavior."

Susannah's grin grew wider. "I'm not sure it's an even deal."

"You drive a hard bargain. I'll throw in the air-conditioning for free."

She looked around the loft. It was the perfect place for her purposes. The fact that Brett had brought her here was significant. He'd made a big concession to her. And he was only asking for one evening of her time in return. "Well, in that case, count me in."

"Good."

Brett walked down the stairs behind Susannah, admiring the way her sundress swished around her athletic-looking calves. It wasn't quite as good as the view going up the stairs had been. But it was still mighty fine, and you couldn't hang a man for looking.

He thought about the plausible-sounding corporate hogwash he'd just dished out. It was true as far as it went. But there was a lot more that he wasn't about to put into words.

Susannah Lindsey was the choicest woman who had shown up in Silver Creek in a long time. He'd been turned on by that great body even before he'd met her. But he'd told himself she'd be all dandelion fluff.

Well, it sure hadn't worked out that way. She'd been the one who'd blown him away. The fun of matching wits with her was enough reason to get friendly with her. But it wasn't the only one. There was a humming between them that he was sure they'd both felt—even before he'd taken her in his arms. And on the dance floor, things had heated up faster than bacon on the griddle. Much as he'd hated to admit it, he'd come to the conclusion that there were some mighty good reasons for getting on Susannah's good side.

But he'd fought the attraction with more stubbornness. In fact, he'd gone looking for evidence to justify his original prejudice. Unfortunately, she'd only impressed him with her spunk.

As they walked back down to the first floor, he was glad she couldn't see the perplexed look on his face. He'd resisted the hooks other women had tried to sink into him. This one seemed to be reeling him in without even trying.

Susannah was thinking about what she'd gotten herself into. "I take it you're making pizzas," she observed.

"Yes."

"What else is on the agenda to keep the troops busy?"

"I've rented a couple of movies."

"Where do you live, and what time do you want me over?" There was still a bit of doubt in her voice.

Brett looked at her. "You're not wondering how to get out of this, are you?"

"A deal is a deal." It wasn't the thought of coping with the kids that was bothering her. Suddenly it had occurred to her that her relationship with Brett had just taken another crazy turn. Usually when favors were called in by associates they had to do with business—putting a good word in with the boss, staying late to help someone finish a proposal or taking over a friend's exercise class for the week. Certainly nothing like helping to referee a kid's birthday party.

"Well then, you just follow the road we're on out of town. When you get to the marina, turn right. I'm a half mile farther down the river. The name's on the mailbox. You'll recognize it anyway."

"Your mailbox?"

"Yeah. The kids are coming at six."

"Then I'll be there at five-thirty to help you with the last-minute details."

For the occasion, Susannah dressed in a comfortable pair of navy culottes and a red-and-white-striped top. She hesitated in front of the mirror, wondering what to do with her hair. A twist seemed too formal. The guys she had dated had always liked it around her shoulders. But this wasn't a date. And she didn't want to give Brett any ideas. The man had enough of those on his own.

Finally she decided to plait her hair into a braid and let it hang over her left shoulder, which was how she often wore it for exercise classes. She tied it with a red ribbon.

As she was leaving the house, one more thought occurred to her. She should bring Billy a gift. But what did you get a twelve-year-old boy?

Then she remembered he liked baseball. On the way to the Tanner house, she stopped at the convenience store and bought fifteen packs of baseball cards and some bright blue paper to wrap them in. Mission accomplished, she took the east road out of town.

She didn't have any trouble following Brett's directions. And she laughed out loud when she saw the mailbox—it was shaped like a fishing creel. His lot was large and heavily wooded with pines, so he had a good deal of privacy. Nestled among the trees was a very modern redwood-and-stone house with lots of glass and sleek angles and decks that looked out over the water. In a corner screened by junipers and rhododendrons was a giant-size hot tub. Again, it wasn't what she'd been expecting. But she was learning to expect the unexpected from Brett Tanner.

Billy threw open the door. "Hi, Miss Lindsey. Thanks for coming. Hey, neat, you brought me something. Thanks."

He set the present down on the hall table. "Dad's in the kitchen cussing over the carrots. You'd better help him." The boy rushed down the hall, and Susannah followed.

She found Brett in a spacious kitchen fitted with cherry-wood cabinets and almond-colored appliances. He was wearing an aqua knit top and khaki Bermuda shorts. But she had only a moment to admire his muscled legs because he looked up accusingly as soon as he spotted her.

"This is all your fault."

"What?"

"You made me feel so guilty about all the junk food I was buying the other night that I decided to add raw vegetables and dip to the menu. But I can't cut these damn carrots right. Either I get little slivers or great big chunks." He held up several examples to prove his point.

Susannah bit back a grin. "Let me," she offered. After washing her hands, she reached for the knife.

"Do you have one without a serrated edge?" she asked.

"Is that the problem?"

"Partly. And your technique."

"No one's ever complained about my technique before," he said, handing her the knife.

Their hands brushed, and Susannah felt a little zing of awareness that she didn't want to feel.

"I like your hair that way. It's cute and sassy." The angry edge to his voice had disappeared.

"Umm."

He stepped away from the built-in cutting board so she could take over.

In a few minutes, she'd dispatched the bag of carrots, a bunch of celery and the cucumbers he'd purchased. She glanced up to find him watching her with an odd look on his face.

"If I ever decide to get into vegetables seriously, I'll know whom to call."

She could handle the teasing Brett better than the one who liked to play up the sexual attraction between them. "Does that mean you want my recipe for zippy carrot salad?"

"Don't hold your breath."

"Were you planning to put the pizzas in the oven soon?" she asked.

"I was going to let the boys run around outside until dark to wear them down a bit."

"If they help us put the pizzas together, that will give them something to do."

"But they're going to be hungry," Brett pointed out.

"Then they'll eat all those nice vegetables while they're waiting."

"You nutrition types are devious, aren't you?"

"Sometimes you gotta be tricky to be effective."

Further conversation was cut short by the doorbell. "Gene's here!" Billy called out. "And so is Joe."

For the next fifteen minutes, the noise got louder and louder, so Brett organized a basketball game in the driveway.

The boys divided up, but the teams were uneven. "Your dad can play with us," Joe declared.

"No fair. He's too good," Billy objected.

"It's just a friendly game," Susannah pointed out, and then wondered whether she should have stepped into the controversy when Billy shot her a sharp look.

A moment later Brett started dribbling the ball. Soon the two teams were at it hot and heavy.

They were all pretty good players. But Susannah found herself watching Brett with the most interest. He was a big man, but he moved with the grace of a natural athlete.

She was particularly drawn to the power in his legs. He had the kind of muscles that a lot of guys spent hours on the weight machines cultivating. But he didn't need a circuit weight-training program to keep in shape.

He lobbed an easy shot over his head. It rolled around the edge of the basket and dropped in.

"Hey, Mr. Tanner, would you coach our basketball team next season?" Gene called out.

"I'll think about it."

After a few more minutes of playing, Brett dropped out of the game and ambled over to where Susannah sat on the steps leading down from the deck.

"You're not too bad, Tanner," she acknowledged as he sat down beside her.

"Billy and I like to go one-on-one after work. Used to be I could wipe him up. Now it's about even. It's sad when you can't keep ahead of a twelve-year-old boy."

"You two seem to have a really good relationship," Susannah remarked.

"I hope so. Losing his mother was tough. One of the reasons I moved back here was so I could spend more time with him."

Susannah imagined it had been hard on him, too. But she suspected he didn't want to pursue the subject.

"Back in Philadelphia I was so busy being a success that I was lucky to make one of his baseball games on the weekends."

Susannah nodded. She could identify with the seductiveness of success. A career could suck up all your time. And what you achieved was never enough. That was one of the reasons she'd jumped at the chance to spend the summer in a place like Silver Creek.

"And now you're the baseball coach," she said, shifting the focus of her thoughts back to Brett.

"Umm-hmm." He stood up and looked over at the boys. "At this age, you've got to feed 'em every two hours or they start gnawing the furniture. So we'd better make sure those pizzas are going to be ready."

Back in the kitchen they both concentrated on work. Brett got out pizza pans; Susannah opened jars of sauce and the packages of cheese and other toppings Brett had purchased.

"Ready for the onslaught?" Brett said.

"I guess."

He leaned out the window. "Come on in and wash your hands, boys."

There was a pounding of tennis shoes on the wooden deck. The stampeding youngsters burst through the door and scattered to the various bathrooms.

Two minutes later, they were all milling around the counters. Susannah put them to work sprinkling on the toppings.

"Mushroom—yuk!" Joe complained.

"Well, do one with no mushrooms."

"Make it one of the first ones."

"Too much cheese, toilet brain." As soon as the words were out of his mouth, the speaker glanced sideways at Susannah.

She shook her head slightly, and he curbed his colorful language a bit from then on. So Brett was right; her presence was toning things down.

They got two pizzas into the oven right away—one with everything and one with just cheese.

As Susannah had predicted, the kids attacked the vegetables and dip with the same enthusiasm they showed for basketball.

Fifteen minutes later they were seated around two tables happily devouring their supper.

Brett and Susannah withdrew to the living room to eat in relative peace. It was a rustic room with oversize furniture, an entertainment center and a large blue mounted fish over the fireplace. The fish wasn't quite to Susannah's taste, but the rest she approved of.

"Do you want your aspirin before or after you eat?" Brett quipped as he set his plate down on the wide plank coffee table and settled into a corduroy-covered chair.

Susannah laughed. "It's not that bad."

"Thank God this only happens once a year."

They smiled at each other as a particularly loud comment bellowed from the other room.

Unaccountably, Susannah felt a little twinge of envy for Brett. Her career was something to be proud of, but there was a whole other dimension to his life that she'd never experienced.

"I'd close the door, but I need to keep an ear out in case the chaos escalates."

"No problem."

Now that the adults were actually out of the room, the boys threw restraint to the wind.

"That's the last piece with no mushrooms, turkey breath."

"So? Pick 'em off another one."

Susannah looked questioningly at Brett.

"Let them work it out," he suggested.

The argument was settled. The boys went on to bragging about their baseball team and razzing each other about everything from girls to haircuts.

Brett had obviously had a lot of practice in tuning out the uproar. He looked relaxed sitting there munching his pizza and sipping from the can of beer he'd gotten out of the refrigerator. But he must have had some kind of parental radar set on low power because the moment a food fight threatened to break out, he was immediately out of his seat and into the other room telling them in a drill-sergeant voice that they were going to have to clean the floor with a toothbrush if they didn't calm down.

They calmed down.

After the meal Billy opened his presents while Susannah and Brett swept all the dinner debris into large garbage bags. Brett had had the foresight to buy all disposable dinnerware, so the cleanup was relatively painless.

When they came back into the family room, Billy looked up. "Thanks for the neat baseball cards, Miss Lindsey."

She noticed he was talking around a wad of gum and that every other boy in the room was also chomping furiously.

"We're having a contest to see who can blow the biggest bubble," Gene informed her.

Susannah looked at Brett again.

He shrugged. "Better than throwing food," he said.

"We saved some gum for you," Billy offered.

"No, thanks."

The bubble-gum contest kept the kids busy for half an hour. Then it was time for the movies Brett had rented.

The boys flopped onto the thick rug in front of the large television set. Susannah settled herself on the couch while Brett loaded the VCR and dimmed the lights.

She was surprisingly worn out. She'd been working hard getting her program off the ground. And the evening with the kids had been wearing, though fun. Susannah closed her eyes. In the next moment, she felt Brett's large body settle down beside her.

"Tired?" he murmured.

Her lids fluttered open. "A little."

"The guys can be a handful."

"It's been a long week."

"All you have to do is settle back and enjoy the movie."

Just then, the title flashed across the screen: *Horror at Hyattsville High, Part Three.*

Susannah sat up straighter. "You didn't tell me it was going to be *this* kind of movie."

"You didn't ask."

She sighed. Horror flicks might be popular with the younger crowd, but so far she'd been able to avoid seeing one. Oh, well, if Billy and his friends could sit through it, so could she. And the rating was PG 13.

It took only a few minutes for her to conclude that the plot was ridiculous. A chemistry experiment gone haywire turned one of the members of the high-school football team from Biff Jekyll into Mr. Hyde. Yet Susannah couldn't help cringing the first time a dead cheerleader fell out of a locker.

Brett gave her a sideways look and settled his arm around her shoulder. She could have protested, but it was no big deal, she told herself. He moved a few inches closer, and she could feel the hairs on his leg as it brushed against her calf. A nice outdoorsy smell came from him.

Susannah could have moved her leg away. She didn't. Instead, she closed her eyes again, ignoring the scenes of mayhem on the screen. There were a dozen chaperons spread out on the carpet in front of the coffee table. This wasn't going to go very far.

Even as she assured herself that she was safe, her senses were jangling from Brett's nearness.

His fingers lightly massaged her shoulder, and she shivered slightly. At the same time, she could feel the warmth radiating from his body. When she slipped lower into the sofa cushions, Brett's cheek settled against the top of her head.

She felt protected as much as anything else. It was a novel sensation. She was a person who was used to fighting her own monsters. And here she was leaning on a man she wasn't even sure she liked.

No, that wasn't exactly fair, part of her muddled brain protested. There were a lot of things she liked about him now that she'd gotten to know him a little better.

Brett slipped his finger under the edge of her sleeve and stroked the silky skin of her upper arm. He liked having Susannah Lindsey on his sofa. He just wished they had a little more privacy. But then if they did, she probably wouldn't be here at all.

He'd been dead set against her when she'd first come to town. But she hadn't let him mow her down. From what he could see, she was a hard worker. And a good sport about helping him out tonight. He wondered what she'd think if she knew how he'd really like to end the evening.

He'd stopped paying attention to the movie a long time ago. Now he couldn't stop himself from brushing his lips against her hair. It smelled so good. And it looked so cute the way she'd braided it to one side.

She sighed and snuggled closer against him.

Unaccountably he felt like a teenager with a date in the last row of the movie theater. He was vividly aware of how close his fingertips were to the top of her breast. Only he wasn't an inexperienced teenage boy, and he knew how exciting it would be to touch her.

She turned her head and looked up at him. In the dim light, his eyes focused on her lips. They parted expectantly in anticipation of his kiss.

Just then, a shriek rang out from one of the boys on the rug. "Ohmygosh! Look at that!"

Chapter Four

Brett and Susannah sprang apart as if they'd just been caught naked in bed.

"Totally gross," Billy shouted.

Susannah's eyes flicked to the screen. The whole football team at Hyattsville High was being buried alive at the town garbage dump.

"Pretty disgusting, all right," she muttered, and glanced at Brett. There was a half-embarrassed, half-amused look on his face.

Susannah put several inches of space on the couch between them. "This has been fun. But I think I'd better be getting home."

"Afraid to stay?"

Was he talking about the movie? Or something else? Instead of asking for clarification, she stood up.

Brett escorted her outside, where it was still a little humid. The night was black, except for the stars. Brett reached back inside the door and flicked on the deck lights. "Watch your step."

He took her arm as she descended and then let go again as they walked down the path to the car. Neither one of them spoke.

"Thanks for helping me out," Brett finally said as she opened the car door.

"Just keeping my end of the bargain."

He studied her face in the light from the car. Her features had taken on a carefully distant expression. His masculine pride wanted to wipe it away. It took a great deal of effort to stifle the impulse to pull her into his arms and cover her lips with his.

A few minutes ago she'd been all ready to kiss him. He'd been surprised and then pleased when she'd gotten so soft and cuddly on the couch beside him. It ticked him off that she was pretending to be so cool and collected now.

But maybe she was right about not getting tangled up with him so precipitously. It could be that his change-about attitude was confusing her. It was sure confusing the dickens out of him. Was he going through some mid-life crisis? Was that why one minute he thought she was an opportunist and the next minute he was the one trying to take advantage of an opportunity? He shook his head in disgust.

Susannah caught the gesture. "What?"

"I was just thinking, you know, when your kid gets to be twelve, it makes you feel kind of ancient."

"If you're appealing to my charitable instincts, you're going to have to do better than that."

He laughed. "I'll have to think up a different approach."

"I can't wait."

"In the meantime, I'll drop the key to the market building in your office tomorrow."

"That will be fine." She got in the car and pulled the door closed.

He stood with his hands on his hips as she backed out of the driveway. No doubt about it, the woman had gotten to him. But he knew he'd gotten to her, too. He wasn't sure where the relationship was heading. But one thing he did know: it wasn't going to be a dull summer.

As she backed down the driveway, Susannah couldn't stop thinking about what might have happened if one of the boys hadn't shrieked. Ancient, indeed! He was the most exciting, virile man she'd cuddled up with in a long time.

There was a potent chemistry between her and Brett that she found hard to resist. But there were a dozen reasons why it wasn't smart to let herself get carried away. She already knew from their brief encounter at the grocery store that gossip spread around Silver Creek like a wildfire in a drought. By tomorrow morning, everybody in town would probably know she'd been at Billy's birthday party. She just hoped the boys had been too wrapped up in the movie to pay any attention to what was going on behind them on the couch.

Of course, it really hadn't been much. And that was the way to keep it. She had a job to do here. She wanted people talking about her program, not the fact that she was falling under the spell of Silver Creek's most eligible bachelor.

There was another thing to consider, too. She was only going to be here for ten weeks, and Brett was firmly entrenched in Silver Creek. That meant there was no future to a relationship between them. So it made sense to keep things between them on a strictly professional level.

Brett must have come to the same conclusion, she decided the next day. He left the key on her desk while she was at lunch, and she didn't see him after that. So much for his different approach! Apparently it was come on strong and then drop 'em like a hot potato when they didn't swoon at his feet.

She told herself she wasn't a bit disappointed. It was better this way. If he wanted to deliberately avoid her, that would just make it easier for her. With a mental shrug, she turned her energies to business.

By the next week, Susannah had several exercise classes going. Donna and Bonnie both joined and volunteered to help her with anything that needed to be done. Susannah was making friends and feeling at home.

Tuesday evening she got a supportive, interested crowd at her first grocery-store cooking demonstration.

"That looks right pretty," Bonnie observed, eyeing Susannah's pineapple-and-carrot salad. "Any chance it'll taste as good as the one Maggie Walker brought to that welcoming party? She always wins first place at the county fair with her recipe."

"I'm not sure what Maggie puts in hers, but this dish is high in vitamins and fiber and very low in calories and fat. You'll have to judge the taste for yourself." Susannah spooned small servings into cups and passed them out.

"Well, this one tastes as good as it looks," Bonnie declared after trying a sample. "Maybe I'll enter it in the fair this summer and beat out old Maggie for the prize."

"I'm glad you liked it."

"So far I've enjoyed everything you've suggested," Nora Mae piped in. "Last night I tried your potato salad, and Dwayne never guessed that I'd replaced some of the mayonnaise with buttermilk."

Susannah winked conspiratorially. "I'll tell you a secret. I know buttermilk's good for me, but I hate the stuff. So when I use it in a recipe, I make sure I can't tell it's there."

"Well, it sure works," Nora Mae enthused.

After the demonstration, Susannah handed out recipes for the annual Memorial Day picnic.

She was so much into the day-to-day activities in Silver Creek it was a surprise when her boss at Healthways called in the middle of the week. "Ready to come back to civilization yet?" Jack inquired.

"I hate to disappoint you, but it's really quite charming here."

"Good. Then it's going to look great on tape."

"On tape?"

"That's right. Cable News called me about doing a feature on us, and I told them we could do some of the filming down there."

Susannah's stomach knotted as she thought about how Brett had reacted to her coming here in the first place. She'd worked hard to convince him she wasn't taking advantage of the town—not that this filming necessarily indicated she was. But she didn't want to jeopardize the progress she'd made—with him or anyone else. She had to sound out the town council before going along with Jack's plans. "Gee, I wish you'd talked to me about it first," she told him.

"I'm telling you about it now."

"Don't go any further with the plans until I get back to you."

"I can't promise."

"Jack!"

"If you insist, I'll hold Cable News off."

"I'd appreciate that."

Susannah hung up, feeling a bit uneasy. Jack wouldn't go ahead with this without her permission, would he?

But before she could stew any more about it, the phone rang again. It was the president of the ladies' auxiliary from the church.

They were putting together several health displays for the annual Memorial Day picnic, and they needed Susannah's input right away or they were going to miss the deadline at the printer. She promised to come right over and look at the material.

The picnic was being held at the park along the riverbank. And on Saturday morning, Susannah put on a pair of cool white shorts and a bright green top and went down early to help set up several booths.

Several hours later, the festive area was bustling. Doc Crowley and his nurse were doing some health-screening tests. Local businesses, who had contributed displays, were handing out discount coupons for everything from healthy foods to running shoes. The ladies' club was selling fresh juices and light snacks. And volunteers were signing up new recruits for Susannah's exercise class. A weigh-in was part of the process, but it was done in private, behind a blanket tied to two trees.

Susannah stopped by Laura Henderson's pottery stand to say hello. She was a dark-haired young woman with a very pretty face and about twenty extra pounds on her body. One of the first people who'd shown up at Susannah's morning exercise class, she'd told Susannah she was determined to lose weight before her tenth high-school reunion, which was coming up in September.

They chatted for a few minutes before Bonnie called Susannah over to the next booth.

"Is this going to be the rage or what?" Bonnie asked, holding up a blue T-shirt with silver lettering. Across the front was emblazoned I Survived the Silver Creek Challenge.

"Let's hope we all survive." Susannah laughed as she bought one and put it in her purse.

At the same booth, the local sporting-goods store was raffling off an exercise bike.

"Five chances for a dollar," the proprietor told her.

Since the money went to charity, Susannah bought a ticket. "I've already got two bikes at home, so if I win, we'll use it at the exercise loft," Susannah said.

The picnic was a new experience for her. There was a sense of community in Silver Creek that she just didn't find in the big city. Everyone knew everyone else. What's more, they knew her. As Susannah moved around the park checking out various activities, she was greeted as a member of the family by almost everyone she encountered.

But one person who didn't come up to her was Brett. Despite her avowed disinterest, she found that she kept looking for him in the crowd. Occasionally she did catch a glimpse of him. He looked trim and athletic in a blue-and-white-striped shirt and cutoffs. She saw him helping the ladies set up, then organize a father-son baseball game. Well, if he didn't want to come up to say hello to her, she wasn't going to chase after him.

At lunchtime Susannah noted that the tables were just as full as they had been when the town had turned out to greet her. But she quickly saw that the two weeks she'd been in town had made a difference.

There wasn't a total shift in eating habits, but a lot of people had used the recipes she'd given out. She recognized her light potato and pasta salads, and there were several bowls of sliced fruit instead of so many sugar-loaded concoctions.

After picking up a plate, Susannah got in line and started making selections.

"The barbecued chicken looks good," a familiar voice observed.

Susannah swiveled around to see Brett standing right behind her. She tried not to look too pleased. But she could feel the corners of her mouth tilting up into a broad welcoming smile.

He grinned back. "I've seen you flitting through the crowd all morning."

"You did?"

"Umm-hmm." He surveyed her shorts and top with his sexy blue eyes. "You're in great shape today."

"It's my business."

"And my pleasure."

"I guess you've been busy, too."

"You noticed."

A flush spread across her cheeks. Now he knew she'd been keeping tabs on him. "Did you work up an appetite?" she asked, changing the subject.

"Of course." As he spoke, he took a generous spoonful of coleslaw and some pasta-tuna salad.

There was a moment's hesitation when they reached the end of the line. Then Brett pointed toward an empty picnic table in the shade of a sweet-gum tree. "Why don't we sit over there?"

Susannah nodded. She hadn't seen or talked to Brett since Billy's birthday party, and now she realized how much she'd missed him. The thought was annoying. She certainly hadn't been sitting around waiting for the man to call. And she wasn't sure how much she liked having him walk right up to her as if they'd just seen each other yesterday.

"How are things working out with the exercise room?" he inquired.

"Fine." The answer came out too tersely.

"Have I done something in particular to make you angry?" he asked.

"Of course not."

"You're not still upset about the way things ended at the party?"

"I wasn't upset."

His eyebrows rose, but instead of commenting, he turned his attention to his plate.

Susannah looked around at the rest of the crowd. There were still plenty of people in line getting food. But nobody brought their plates over to their table, even though it still had six empty places. Then it dawned on her. Everybody must have assumed they wanted to be alone.

Just then she spotted Donna's mop of red hair in the crowd. She and her husband, Charlie, were looking for an empty seat. Susannah stood up and waved.

Donna hesitated. Charlie came lumbering over.

"I always do like a good picnic," he observed as he sat down.

"You don't mind if we join you?" Donna asked.

"We'd love some company," Susannah assured her.

Charlie had started tackling his plate with enthusiasm. "They've got some right tasty new dishes this year," he said between mouthfuls.

"Thanks to Susannah's recipes," Donna told him. She looked across the table. "I brought your gazpacho salad."

"I had some. It turned out great," Susannah responded.

"You know, if the food's this good at the Fourth of July picnic, nobody will even miss the fireworks," Donna remarked.

Brett rolled his eyes and Charlie coughed.

Susannah had the feeling that she was listening to the punch line of a private joke. Before she could ask what they were talking about, Charlie changed the subject.

"How's the fishing business?" he asked Brett.

"Hectic. I've been working till after dark every night trying to get my big cruiser fixed up before that charter group comes in next week."

He'd relayed the information to Charlie, but Susannah suspected it was as much for her benefit. So he had been busy. Still, that didn't explain why he hadn't at least called her.

The conversation turned to more general topics. With the other couple acting as a buffer, Susannah found herself able to relax in Brett's company.

After a suitable interval, the mayor rang a large cowbell. "The afternoon contests are about to start."

In the frenzy of her own preparations, Susannah had forgotten about the afternoon games. Now she remembered that they were fund-raisers—bets being placed on the outcome of various events and all the money going to local charities—and that she'd agreed to participate.

"I wonder what they signed me up for," she murmured to Donna.

The other woman looked a bit flustered and didn't quite meet her eye. "Nora Mae has the list. But don't worry about it; they'll call your name."

Susannah wanted to ask more questions, but just then Billy came rushing over to get some money from his father so he could make some bets.

He gave Susannah a lopsided grin. "Reckon you'll be in at least one of the big races."

"I can hardly wait."

"It's fun." Without elaborating, he stuffed some dollar bills into his pocket and dashed off to join his friends again.

Susannah and Brett got up with the rest of the crowd and strolled over to a grassy field where the competitions would take place. Everybody was in high spirits. Apparently this was one of the features of the picnic that Silver Creek really looked forward to.

There was a lot of laughter when the names were called for the egg-tossing contest. It was all in good fun, but apparently the committee had gone out of its way to pick unlikely contestants. The minister and his wife. The local beautician and the president of the bank. The head librarian and the elementary-school principal. Some of the people selected didn't look too excited about being chosen. But they were all good sports about it.

Each team of two had to toss a raw egg back and forth—getting farther and farther apart. Anyone who missed was likely to have a quick egg shampoo. By the time the bank president and the beautician claimed victory, the course was spattered with raw eggs. And spectators were laughing so hard that their sides hurt.

For the next event everyone moved to a new location while the volunteer fire department cleaned up the field. Susannah was just thanking her lucky stars that she hadn't been picked for the egg toss when Mayor Rollins announced the next event—the three-legged race.

"We've got a real hot match for this one," Dwayne said. "Our last year's champion, Brett Tanner, and—" there was an expectant hush, and Susannah had a sinking feeling in her stomach "—and the lovely Miss Susannah Lindsey."

She shot Donna an accusing look; the redhead just shrugged. Susannah was tempted to fade back into the crowd. But someone behind her gave her a little nudge, and she reluctantly stepped forward. "But I've never done anything like this before," she protested.

She glanced over at Brett, wondering if he'd had anything to do with this. But from the bemused expression on his face, she knew that he was just as surprised as she.

He recovered quickly, however. "The first time may not be the best, but it's sure exciting," he promised with a twinkle in his eye.

Susannah still had her doubts, but there was no way to back out gracefully, not with everybody in town watching.

They were going to be racing against the fire chief and one of the gym teachers, the star quarterback and the head cheerleader, and a number of other athletic types.

"The competition looks tough," Brett observed as Bonnie tied his left leg to Susannah's right one.

"Tell me if it's too tight," Bonnie instructed.

Susannah had no complaint about that, but she noticed immediately that she couldn't move her leg without rubbing against Brett's. If she'd known, she would have worn slacks instead of shorts. Now she could feel every hair on his leg as though they were charged with electricity.

"We've gotta move the bound legs like they belong to one person," Brett instructed.

They certainly felt as though they belonged to one person, all right, Susannah thought.

"We'd better practice," he muttered, his voice sounding a bit husky.

They quickly discovered that the best way to stay upright was for each of them to anchor an arm firmly at the other's waist.

Susannah could feel the imprint of Brett's fingers through the fabric of her knit top, damp from the high temperature and clinging to her ribs. Worse, her own hand was receiving just as vivid an impression of his rock-hard torso.

Susannah knew her face was red, and not just from the sun. She glanced down the field toward the halfway mark. It was over fifty yards away. And they'd have to turn around and come back. "Do you think we can really make it?" she asked.

"Last year I made it with Bonnie. If I can't make it with you, I won't be able to hold my head up at the next council meeting."

Susannah ignored the suggestive remark. "Who were you running against?"

"The undertaker and his wife."

Susannah had met them. Neither looked very fast. Apparently, this year someone had decided to beef up the competition. It suddenly dawned on her that since she was the town's new physical-fitness leader, she'd better make a good showing.

The race was almost ready to begin. Susannah could see grinning faces in the crowd as she and Brett hobbled up to the starting line. She spotted Billy. He'd been smiling before, but now, to her surprise, he looked about as embarrassed as she felt. The thought crossed her mind that perhaps he didn't like seeing her paired so intimately in public with his dad.

And they couldn't have been much more intimate unless they'd been alone together.

"On your mark. Get set. Go!" A whistle blew, and the participants started off.

Susannah didn't know how Brett had managed with Bonnie. Maybe he'd half carried her. But after a couple of steps into the race, it was obvious that the event had brought out his competitive spirit. He was determined to win.

"Damn! We've got to move together," Brett muttered. "You've got to get the rhythm right."

"Me?"

"Up, down, up, down," he chanted the cadence for her.

She would have laughed if he hadn't been so serious. They were in second place, right behind the quarterback and the cheerleader. The kids had youth on their side, but Brett had determination. Susannah realized that the best way to proceed was to match her movements to his. Once she let him take charge, they pulled into the lead.

"That's good, honey," he puffed. "You just gotta keep up with me."

She gave aerobics classes five days a week, and she suspected she could run him into the ground if she wanted. But this was hardly the time to argue about who had more stamina.

On the other hand, she didn't do aerobics with her leg tied to Brett's. Her heart was pounding, and her breath was coming in ragged little pants. And she could hear Brett's labored breathing as well.

They made the turn at the bank of trees ahead of the other couples. Now they were in the home stretch and in the lead. Susannah had gotten caught up in the excitement. It wasn't just the race. It was Brett.

The crowd had started to urge them on.

Just then, Susannah's foot hit a tree root, and she stumbled. Brett's arm tightened on her waist. He practically lifted her off the ground on the next two steps.

"Almost there, honey," he huffed. "Don't stop now."

She gritted her teeth and concentrated on the rhythm that Brett was setting. Another couple pounded the ground right behind them. Susannah resisted the urge to glance over her shoulder, knowing that would slow her down.

She and Brett clung tightly together. His fingers dug into her ribs, but she didn't notice. Their skin glistened with a fine sheen of perspiration. Their bodies moved as one.

The finish line was directly ahead of them. In a final burst of energy, they surged across, each panting and gasping and grinning.

The crowd was cheering wildly around them.

"That was wonderful," Brett breathed. "*You* were wonderful."

Susannah nodded, not quite able to take his words in. The race was over, but she couldn't explain the feeling of exhilaration that was still throbbing through her veins. It wasn't just the sweet thrill of victory.

Still bound together, they turned and stared at each other. People crowded around them, offering congratulations. They hardly noticed.

The focus of Susannah's attention had narrowed to one man—Brett Tanner. She was taking in a whole host of suddenly fascinating details about him, like the way his damp hair clung to his forehead and the feel of his strong muscles under her fingers. His blue eyes were gazing down into her brown ones with a questioning intensity that sent little zings of awareness along her nerve endings.

For a moment it seemed that neither one of them was capable of moving. Finally, Brett's face lowered and Susannah's tilted up.

Her eyes fluttered closed as his lips covered hers. It was their first kiss, but there was nothing tentative about it. Brett's lips moved over hers—strong, sure and assertive. The kiss of a conquering male claiming his due after the hard-fought battle.

But this wasn't like days of old when all the glory had been for the male. Susannah shared in it equally, claiming her own spoils of victory and kissing him back with just as much exuberance.

His strong arms went around her body, gathering her close. She gave an involuntary little sigh of pleasure. Automatically her body molded itself to Brett's.

Susannah's head spun, and she clung to the broad expanse of Brett's shoulders to anchor herself. She was in danger of getting high on the taste and touch of the man who held her so tightly in his embrace.

"Go for it, boy!"

"Right on."

The enthusiastic words were followed by several loud whistles of raucous approval.

Dimly, voices penetrated the pleasant fog that swirled in Susannah's mind. Her eyes snapped open, and she blinked in the bright sunshine. In the next second the scene bounced back into focus. She was standing in the middle of a crowd of cheering, whistling residents of Silver Creek and kissing the town's most eligible bachelor.

Susannah felt her face flame. Never in her life had she been caught in such a public display of emotions. Automatically, her hands came up to press against Brett's chest. He continued to hold her fast as he stared down at her, his eyes dark with passion.

"Brett," she whispered.

Finally he, too, must have realized exactly where they were. He shook his head as if to clear it before releasing Susannah.

"Y'all must be mighty pleased about winning," someone in the crowd observed.

Susannah was rarely at a loss for words, but her mind had gone completely blank. At the moment all she could do was wish that the earth would open up and swallow her. She'd never been more embarrassed in her life.

Brett apparently had more presence of mind. He met the townspeople's grins with one of his own. "We sure are," he drawled.

But any pretense to suaveness was spoiled when he tried to take a casual step back from Susannah and almost landed on his seat in the dirt. He'd apparently forgotten all about his leg still being bound to his partner's. Arms flailing, he struggled to stay on his feet. But he also knocked Susannah off balance in the process.

She gasped and grabbed wildly for his shoulder to steady herself. For a minute they teetered wildly. By some miracle they both finally regained their footing.

There was another chorus of hearty laughter around them.

"Watch it, boy. You ain't exactly shut of her yet!" someone called out.

That brought another whoop of hilarity.

Ignoring the good-natured heckling, Brett leaned down and began to untie the cords that bound them together. Susannah simply stood there with her arms folded across her chest, staring off into space. When she caught a flash of movement out of the corner of her eye, she turned to see Billy striding rapidly away across the field.

From the way his head was bent—and memories of her own teenage tendency toward embarrassment—Susannah suspected that he hadn't much liked what he'd just seen. Probably he was mortified that his father had just made a fool of himself.

Before she could say anything to Brett, someone came over and clapped her on the back. She looked up to see Dwayne grinning at her. She managed a weak smile in return.

"That was mighty thrillin'. Thanks for being such a good sport," the mayor said. "We haven't had that much excitement here in a long spell."

"Oh, uh, not at all," she replied, hoping he was referring to the race.

Brett had finally freed their legs, and Susannah took a grateful step away from him. To give herself something to do, she leaned down to massage her skin where the rope had bitten into it. Looking up from under lowered lashes, she was glad to see they were no longer the center of attention. The crowd was listening eagerly to the announcement of the next contest—a water-balloon relay.

Brett put his hand on Susannah's arm. "You all right?" he asked.

"You and I have to talk."

"About what?"

"Your son, for one thing. I just saw him stalking away from that little performance we put on."

Brett's face clouded, and he looked over his shoulder. But Billy was nowhere in sight. "I'll catch him later."

"Billy isn't the only thing we have to talk about."

Brett seemed to have recovered his equanimity. "Shoot."

"Not here. In private."

He shrugged and looked around at the crowd. "Well, there isn't much of that around here. But you're welcome to drop by my house anytime."

She hadn't been prepared for the invitation. Before she could answer, he said, "I just spotted Billy," and without waiting for a reply, left her standing in the middle of the field.

Chapter Five

Susannah didn't see Brett for the rest of the afternoon. But a lot of other people at the picnic made a point of letting her know they'd seen the exhibition after the race. Some made teasing remarks. Others were content with a sly look. It was obvious they were thinking more about her personal affairs than the project she'd been hired to lead. She wished they would just forget about the kiss.

She was feeling a bit weary as she said goodbye to the Nevinses and climbed into her car. But she couldn't stop her mind from analyzing the situation. When she'd agreed to come to Silver Creek, she hadn't thought about the fishbowl aspect of life in a small town. It was definitely a force to be reckoned with. All the talk about her and Brett was going to take something away from her professional effectiveness.

She pulled into her driveway and climbed the steps to the front porch of the cottage. It was almost six in the evening.

Maybe she was overreacting. After all, it had been just a kiss. Maybe it wouldn't seem so momentous after she watched the evening news.

The lead story about a plane hijacking in the Middle East helped put her own little problems in perspective. But she sat up straighter when the commentator started talking about a state politician who was not seeking reelection because of a scandal with a beautiful young campaign worker. He'd been protesting that the woman was a friend of his wife and that what had happened between them was innocent. But then some hotshot reporter had produced a picture of them kissing.

Susannah cringed. Someone could have taken a picture of her and Brett this afternoon. She could just see it plastered across the front page of the *Silver Creek Banner*. Of course, she reminded herself, neither one of them was married. But that didn't lessen the local interest. Or the potential damage to her effectiveness.

Susannah stood up and began pacing back and forth in front of the television set. She wanted to have this out with Brett tonight, not wait until tomorrow. Crossing to the phone, she looked up Brett's number and dialed. It was busy. When she tried again a few minutes later, it still was.

At least she knew he was home. And he had invited her to drop in anytime. In Atlanta she wouldn't have dreamed of just showing up at somebody's house. But this was Silver Creek, where everything was a lot more casual. Maybe she'd just take Brett up on his invitation.

As she was picking up her purse from the table near the front door, she caught a glimpse of herself in the mirror. Her hair had come out of its neat braid, and her clothes were rumpled. Hating herself for caring about what she looked like, she nevertheless went back to her bedroom and changed into dark slacks and a crisp cotton shirt.

Before leaving, Susannah gave the phone one more try. Still busy.

It was just getting dark as she pulled into Brett's driveway and parked behind the silver pickup truck. There was a light on in the house, but when Susannah knocked, no one answered.

"Brett? Are you there?" she called.

"I'm around back."

She followed a walkway around the house to where the deck widened out. The lights were dim, and she didn't immediately see anyone.

"Over here."

At the sound of his deep voice, she whirled and found herself facing the hot tub. In the light from the living room she could make out Brett's head and bare shoulders above the bubbling water. He sat up straighter, and she saw his chest was covered with a crinkly mat of blond hair.

"What are you doing?"

"Soaking my aching muscles. I think I overdid it this afternoon."

"I think you did."

He lifted a can of beer and took a slow swallow as he regarded her from under half-lowered lids.

Susannah noticed that he didn't make any other effort to move. The lack of concern made her bristle. "I told you at the picnic that we had to talk. Do you expect me to have a conversation with you while you're lounging in the water like that?"

He grinned, enjoying some private joke.

Susannah planted her hands on her hips. "Well?"

"Honey, I could always climb out. But to tell the truth, I'm not exactly dressed for company." He shrugged.

Suddenly she realized that he must be sitting there in the buff. "On second thought, don't get up on my account," she told him hastily.

His grin widened. "Tell you what. If you throw me that robe over on the bench, I'll put it on."

Susannah fetched the robe and averted her eyes as she approached the side of the tub. After handing the garment to Brett, she primly turned her back to him.

Behind her she could hear the water sloshing as he stood up. Despite the fact that she'd come out here to tell him there wasn't going to be a repeat of the afternoon's performance, she found herself imagining what he looked like with water streaming down his well-muscled body. That wasn't difficult after they'd been so intimately entwined just a few hours earlier.

"I'm decent now."

The words came from very close to her ear, and she jumped. Turning around, she saw Brett was drying his hair with a towel. When he finished, he lowered himself onto the bench that was built into the deck railing.

The robe hit him midthigh. He started to cross his legs, then thought better of it.

Well, he might be covered up, Susannah thought, but this certainly wasn't the way she'd envisioned conducting this particular conversation—or any other.

He'd brought his beer along and gestured with the can toward the other end of the bench. "You might as well be comfortable. Drink?"

"No, thanks." She wanted him to understand that this wasn't a social call.

"What did you want to talk about?"

She was going to have to get right to the point. "That kiss this afternoon."

He shook his head. "Yeah, that was really something, wasn't it?"

"Yes. I mean, no."

"Shook you up, too, huh?"

"It shook you up?"

"Couldn't you tell?"

This wasn't going at all the way Susannah had planned.

"Listen, Brett Tanner, I've never been more embarrassed in my life. I'm not the kind of woman who makes a public spectacle of herself."

"You mean you'd like to try again in private?" There was an amused note in his voice. He was enjoying this, damn him.

"No. That's not what I mean," Susannah hurriedly answered, wondering how to get through his supreme male confidence. "You know everybody in town is talking about us," she went on in a somewhat calmer voice.

"So?"

"So that's not helping my professional image. And I've got to maintain my dignity if my program is going to have any chance of succeeding."

He smoothed the sash of his robe contemplatively between his thumb and forefinger. "I can understand how you feel."

"You can?"

He nodded. "I never noticed it so much growing up. But when I moved back here after being away for a while, it was a big adjustment to realize how wrapped up people in a small town are in each other's lives."

"So then we have to let people know we're not interested in each other."

He laughed and moved a little closer to her on the bench. "Honey, you start running around protesting that we're not doing anything, and everybody will assume the worst."

"They will?"

"Of course. I know my friends are getting a kick out of matchmaking. I've found the best way to handle it is to go along with it. That way, public interest fizzles out."

"You really think so?"

"Umm-hmm."

"But what about—" Susannah never got a chance to finish the sentence.

"I think we'd better find out first if there's any truth behind the gossip," he interrupted. "It could have just been the thrill of winning the race, you know."

There was a wry note in his voice. He'd issued a challenge. And to tell the truth, she was curious, too. She'd never lost control with a man the way she had this afternoon. Had it just been the thrill of victory?

Her heart started to pound, but she didn't turn her face away as his head bent toward hers. Her hands anchored themselves on his broad shoulders. Just a kiss. She could handle that, she told herself, looking up defiantly into the deep blue of his eyes. She really believed that until the moment Brett's lips touched hers.

It was just the way it had been after the race. Compelling. Engulfing. Overwhelming.

Her eyelids fluttered closed as his lips moved over hers, and she felt her blood racing through her veins. No, it wasn't exactly like this afternoon. Now that they were alone in the secluded darkness, she was even more wrapped in the sensual web that seemed to be weaving itself around them.

Her lips parted under his, unconsciously begging for more intimate contact. When his tongue swept into her mouth, she murmured her pleasure.

He growled a response deep in his throat and pulled her up so that she was sitting in his lap.

She had never responded so powerfully to a man before. And she wanted more. Without any thought, her fingers splayed across his cheek, taking delight in the slightly rough texture of his beard. Her other hand found the vee where the folds of his robe crossed and slipped inside. She paused for a moment, feeling the racing of his heart under her palm. It matched the frantic thudding inside her own chest.

Then she buried her fingers in the thick hair of his chest, and he shuddered.

Somehow that very primitive reaction brought a shred of sanity back to Susannah. Or maybe it was the sudden remembrance that Brett wasn't wearing anything under his robe. What's more, she had come here to tell him they had to stop giving Silver Creek something to talk about, and she'd ended up in his arms.

"Brett, no."

He pulled her more tightly to him. "Yes."

"No," she repeated. "Stop. We can't."

His lips lingered on hers for a moment and then moved to chart a sensual path across her cheek. It ended at her ear, where he began to trace the delicate whorls with his tongue. "Why not? We're both adults. We both want this."

Reason was fleeing again. He was right. Yes, why not? she wondered. Then she remembered a small, hunched figure stalking away from the picnic. "Billy. He might come out here."

"He's not home. A bunch of the guys are spending the night at a slumber party."

"But he was pretty upset this afternoon, wasn't he?" Susannah persisted.

She felt Brett stiffen. "Yeah," he answered.

For a moment he didn't move. Then he sighed and shifted Susannah off his lap.

She had asked him to stop. Now she couldn't quite bear to break the contact. She laid her head against Brett's chest. "Do you want to tell me about it?"

He sighed again. "Billy and I have been alone for a long time. I've gotten out of the habit of having anyone to discuss problems with."

"If you don't want to talk about it..."

"No. I do."

She looked up at him. His brow was furrowed. "I caught up with him just as he was climbing on his bike. He wasn't going to let me say anything."

"I remember how it was when I was a kid and my parents did something that I thought was stupid," she offered.

"Yeah. Me, too." He twirled his robe's sash between his fingers. "Billy didn't want to listen. I had to grab the handlebars and stop him from pedaling away."

"What did he say?"

Brett laughed. "Nothing. He just glared at me. So I asked him if he was embarrassed seeing me kiss you in front of everybody. He said the whole town was laughing at me."

"What did you say?"

Brett looked uncomfortable for a moment. "Guy talk, you know."

"Like what?" She had the suspicion she wasn't going to like what she heard.

"I told him men don't laugh at a guy who takes what he wants from a beautiful woman; they envy him."

Susannah sat up straighter and moved away from him. "Well, that's certainly a pretty macho interpretation of events. Takes what he wants? Is that how you saw what happened?"

"I was trying to put it in terms he'd understand."

Susannah cocked her head to one side.

"Dammit, I wasn't exactly taking. It was what *you* wanted, too. You were sure kissing me back—in front of everybody."

There was no use denying it, Susannah thought. Yes, she'd certainly kissed him back. And she knew that she'd been kidding herself a few moments ago. Almost from the first minute she and Brett had laid eyes on each other, they'd been heading toward something explosive—like the way that kiss had just leaped out of control between them. And like now, when he'd taken her in his arms again.

"Brett," she said in a low voice, "despite the way I've been acting with you, I'm not the kind of woman who gets into casual affairs."

"I know that."

"Then what are we doing?"

"I'm not feeling very casual about you." His voice was husky.

"But I'm only going to be in Silver Creek for the summer. You live here, and I live in Atlanta."

"Atlanta's on the same continent."

"But—"

"Let's not worry about the end of the summer until then."

"I have to."

For a moment he didn't say anything. Then he started to speak in a contemplative voice. "You know, I had the wrong idea about you right from the beginning. I thought you were a sexy, empty-headed babe out to make a buck off Silver Creek. Well, you're sexy all right, but you're also pretty darn sharp. And you've got integrity. I was sort of waiting to see if a bunch of media types from the big city showed up at the picnic this afternoon. But you sure didn't try to capitalize on us."

"I told you I wasn't going to do that."

"I know. I guess I had to find out for myself." He reached out and took her hand. "Susannah, I haven't met anyone like you in a long time."

"Like what?"

He stroked his thumb across her knuckles. "Anyone who attracted me as much—physically and every other way."

A little shiver went up her arm. If she were honest, she'd admit that no one had ever attracted her this much, either. She turned her face up and stared into Brett's midnight eyes. "Brett—"

"Shh." He leaned over and brushed his lips very lightly against hers. "We can just—"

They were interrupted by the slamming of the back door. A moment later Billy pounded out onto the deck.

"Dad, I came home to get my flashlight. Joe is setting up a tent in the backyard, and—" He stopped short when he saw the two adults sitting next to each other on the bench. "Oh, uh, I didn't know—"

"It's all right, son."

"I came over to talk to your dad," Susannah interjected quickly.

Billy studied the adults on the bench with interest. "Yeah. Well."

Susannah got to her feet. "We were just finishing up."

Brett gave her a long look. She knew he wanted to continue the conversation, but she needed to distance herself from him.

"I'll talk to you tomorrow," he finally said when she didn't waver.

"All right."

While Billy was still standing out on the deck, she turned and left.

"Ready to get started?" Susannah asked.

There were groans from several of the fifteen women assembled in the loft.

"After last time, I've been wonderin' if you're related to Attila the Hun," Bonnie said. There was a chorus of agreement around the room.

Susannah laughed. "The more you do it, the easier it gets."

Laura Henderson stood up. "You know, my muscles hurt, muscles I didn't even know I had. But I'm already seeing some results," she said, and then did a quick twirl for the rest of the class.

"Good for you."

Laura had turned out to be the most dedicated of Susannah's supporters. She came to exercise class three times a week and was faithfully using the recipes Susannah had given out. And beyond the instructor-student relationship, the two of them had become friends.

Laura was a gifted potter who supported herself by selling the bowls and tableware she created. She'd stayed in Silver Creek after high school to take care of her aging father. He had died last winter, and now Laura wasn't sure where she wanted to live. She and Susannah had had several conversations about the difference between small-town and big-city life.

But the one thing Laura focused on was the class reunion. Susannah suspected there was someone special in Laura's life who was coming back to town for the event.

The music started, and Susannah clapped her hands. "All right, let's go to it."

She led the group into a slow and easy warm-up routine. Once their muscles were stretched, they moved into a fast-paced dance number.

Fifty minutes later, Susannah wiped a bead of perspiration off her forehead. "You're doing great. Hang in there for a little bit longer," she urged.

The music slowed, and Susannah began her cool-down routine of graceful stretching. When it was over, several of the women flopped down on the mats.

Susannah crossed to the tape deck and turned it off. When she glanced up at the doorway, she saw Brett, with just a bit of hair visible above the first button of his tan open-necked shirt. It was enough to remind her of how sexy he'd looked lazing in the hot tub.

She was suddenly very aware of her own raspberry-colored leotard plastered to her body by perspiration. To give herself something to do, she tucked a strand of damp hair into the bun at the back of her neck. "You could have come in and joined us," she offered. Then they'd be on an even footing right now, she thought.

"It was more fun to watch—you." He didn't bother to hide the twinkle in his eye.

Her pulse should have returned to normal during the cool-down period. She was sure it was still up to her aerobic rate. She looked around. More than one of her students were grinning. So much for damping the rumors they'd started at the picnic.

"See you around. You two have fun, now," Laura tossed over her shoulder as she stepped out of the room.

Usually some of the students stayed to talk. But now they all followed Laura's example and scurried downstairs until only Susannah and Brett were left in the exercise room.

"What are you doing here?" she finally asked.

"I own the place, remember?"

"Oh, right. I forgot."

"You looked even better than on that tape. Do you give private lessons?"

The thought of working Brett into the ground was appealing. But she shook her head. A one-to-one workout in close quarters was asking for trouble.

"Too bad. Then how about a baseball game?"

"I don't play."

"I mean watch."

"I'm sorry, but I have to take a shower, and then I've got my first call-in radio program."

"Oh, you do? Well, I didn't mean right now. I meant at five." He leaned back against the wall and crossed his legs at the ankles. "If you want to understand Silver Creek psychology, you ought to come see one of our major summer attractions."

What she ought to do was stay away from this man, she told herself. Instead she asked, "Are you coaching?"

He nodded. "Come on. It'll be fun. And you can show everybody how you can resist kissing me after we win!"

"Brett, you're terrible!"

"That's what they all say."

She looked up at him. She'd been handling big-city, predatory males for years. She could probably think of something so cutting to say that he'd turn on his heel and go away and leave her alone. But she knew in her heart that she didn't want him to do that.

Their conversation at his house hadn't really resolved anything. But somehow it made a difference. Maybe it was what he'd said about feeling serious about her. Or maybe it was her response to the kiss.

At any rate, she found herself wanting to know the man better, to find out if there was anything solid to the relationship once the flash fire burned itself out.

She'd never met anyone who'd given up a prestigious corporate job to buy a marina. She wanted to see him working there, to understand why it was important to him.

And she wanted to see him coaching the Silver Creek Little League team. He was probably an excellent coach, if the way he'd handled the birthday party was any indication.

"At five?" she asked.

"Umm-hmm. The field is right next to the park where we had the picnic."

"Oh, it is?"

"Don't back out."

* * *

An hour and a half later, Susannah reported to the studios of WSIL, which operated out of a converted gas station on Main Street.

"The engineer's wife went into labor. So I'm going to do that job and host the show, too," Dave Caldwell explained.

"Would it be easier just to play some music this afternoon?" Susannah asked.

"Oh, no. We've been doing promos for you all last week. And we've got four advertisers signed up. We gotta go with it." He motioned toward a small soundproof room with two microphones and two chairs. "Let me show you the setup. I'll screen the calls so nobody'll embarrass you over the air with a question about whether sex is good exercise."

"In Silver Creek?"

"We've been known to get some doozies. Watch the board in front of you," Dave told her. "If the red lights are on, that means we have some calls. If not, just keep talking."

Susannah rolled her eyes. "I hope we get some calls."

"You'll do fine—whatever happens."

After a commercial for Parker's Feed and Grain Store, Susannah began with a five-minute prepared talk on what she hoped the listeners would get out of the programs. "I'll be glad to address all your questions about exercise and nutrition," she told her radio audience. "If I don't know an answer, I'll look it up and get back to you next time."

To Susannah's relief, the board indicated four incoming calls.

"You're on the air," Dave told the first caller.

"Hey there, Miss Lindsey."

Even though the caller didn't identify himself, she recognized the voice right away. It was Dwayne. He sounded a little bit self-conscious.

"An exercise program doesn't have to be fancy, does it? I read an article in one of those grocery-store newspapers about exercise," he went on. "It said walking every day will keep the doctor away. Is that right?"

"Well, walking is good aerobic exercise if you do it briskly. If it's your only main source of exercise, you should do it at least three times a week. Try for a fifteen-minute mile. And work up to several miles a day."

Out at the marina, Brett glanced at his watch. Darn. He'd been so busy checking out the engine that had just been overhauled that he'd almost forgotten Susannah's radio program. After jumping down from the deck of the twenty-footer to the dock, he tied the rope around a wood piling, then turned on the portable radio he'd brought from the office.

He stopped for a moment and listened. Over the air, Susannah had a nice soothing, yet professional voice. If she was nervous, you couldn't tell. The mayor had just asked her about walking. So much for a romantic stroll in the moonlight, Brett thought. Even if she agreed to go with him, she'd probably insist that they do it at a trot.

The next anonymous caller was Bonnie. "Is it really a lot better to eat poultry instead of red meat?"

"Well," Susannah began, "most of the fat in chicken is in the skin or right under it. So if you pull the skin off, you're getting rid of a lot of the fat. Three ounces of chicken have 150 calories. And three ounces of lean red meat have about 390 calories. But I can't recommend either duck or goose. They're both very high in fat. But even a weight-loss diet can include a modest portion of lean beef a couple of times a week."

Brett sauntered toward the office carrying the radio. Too bad, he thought, he wouldn't be able to barbecue steak if he wanted Susannah to come for dinner after the game. And his hunting buddies were going to be real sad to hear about the goose and duck.

A lot of the normal ordinary things you did to get to know a woman just wouldn't work with her. But that did make her more of a challenge!

"Does exercising too much give women those big bulging muscles like weight lifters have?" The caller was Donna. Susannah sighed. Apparently the town council was also worried about whether the show was going to get any calls. They must have been up all night thinking of questions to ask her.

"No," Susannah answered. "Women can develop shapely, well-defined muscles without becoming muscle-bound. That's because we just don't have high enough levels of the male hormone testosterone to get the muscles men do."

Brett settled back in his office chair and propped his feet up on the desk. At last Susannah had gotten to a topic he could appreciate. She seemed as well-informed about male hormones as she was about carrot juice. He wondered what she'd do, he thought with a wicked grin, if he called up and asked if sex were good exercise. Of course, Dave would probably keep a question like that off the air. Maybe they could do some personal research on the subject.

* * *

Doc Crowley rounded out the town council's contribution to Susannah's radio debut with a question about getting a doctor's okay before starting on a strenuous exercise program. After that, the switchboard stayed lit until the end of the program.

"That was great," Dave told her.

"Did you know that just about everyone on the town council was going to be calling in?"

He looked a bit embarrassed. "Mayor Rollins might have mentioned something about it this morning."

She shook her head. "If you'd just told me, I wouldn't have been worried about getting a response."

"Oh, yeah."

"Well, it was a good way to get things rolling. And I'm looking forward to next week—same time, same place."

Chapter Six

It was five-fifteen before Susannah got to the ball field. The bleachers were already full of parents, and the two teams were receiving last-minute instructions before starting to play.

Billy's team was called the Silver Creek Cardinals. They wore red-and-white uniforms like the St. Louis Cardinals, only theirs advertised Tanner's Marina across the back. So Brett had paid for the outfits. His own shirt was identical. But the boys must have given it to him as a joke because it said Pop Fly on the back.

Clipboard in hand, he was assigning boys to various positions. He had a few private words for each one and a slap on the back as they left to take their places.

Some of the women Susannah had met around town had sons on the team. When they saw her, they made a place for her on one of the benches.

"Taking in the big-time sports, I see," Mary Sue Williams observed.

"Guess I am."

"I think she came to check out the coach," Jeanette Baker teased. She and Mary Sue were in one of Susannah's exercise classes.

Susannah took Brett's advice and ignored the comment. "Do you come to all the games?" she asked the group.

"Wouldn't miss it," Mary Sue told her. "My son, Danny, is the starting pitcher," she added. Then she grinned. "I have to warn you that we get a little hepped up when anybody from our team gets on base."

Silver Creek was playing the Osborn Pirates, who were wearing orange and black. They were up at bat first. Susannah had been to see the Atlanta Braves play a few times. There was the same kind of excitement in the crowd as the umpire yelled "Batter up!"

Danny was a good pitcher, and the infield was excellent. It took only ten minutes for the Cardinals to get the Pirates out in the first inning. They did it with good pitching and a neat double play from Billy, who played shortstop.

Brett gave a whoop as his boys came up to bat. And the mothers started chanting "We want a hit. We want a hit."

The boys coolly ignored the hoopla. Susannah watched them strut up to the plate like the big leaguers; she could tell that they'd been well coached.

When they made a good play or got a hit, Brett shouted his approval from the sidelines. "Nice throw. Good base running. Way to hit it!"

She watched them glow under his praise. Even when the ball went between their legs or they struck out, Brett was there with the encouraging words that they'd do better next time up.

"How many innings do they play?" Susannah asked Mary Sue at the end of the fifth.

"Six. This is really going to be close. Cross your fingers. Their slugger is coming up now."

Susannah hadn't realized the game was almost over. As anxiously as any of the parents, she focused her attention on the players. The Pirates were batting. There was a close call at home plate, with a player sliding in on a cloud of dust. The umpire called "Safe."

Brett jumped to his feet and stomped over. "Safe? What do you mean, 'safe'?" he bellowed.

"Safe," the umpire repeated.

Brett threw his cap to the ground. "He was out by a mile."

But the umpire wasn't going to change his decision. And Brett went back to the bench.

Susannah could feel his frustration. She wanted to go over and put her hand on his shoulder. But she couldn't do that in front of all these people. She had the feeling it wasn't appropriate anyway.

By the time Silver Creek came to bat in the bottom of the sixth inning, the score was tied. Susannah's mouth was so dry she could barely swallow. If anybody had told her she would get so involved in a kids' baseball game, she would have laughed. But when Mary Sue clutched her arm, she clutched back.

The Cardinals were down to their last out, with Billy and Danny on base. There was a wild pitch, and the catcher missed the ball. From the sidelines, Brett gave a signal.

"What's he doing?" Susannah leaned over and whispered.

"Ohmygosh, they're going to try a double steal," Mary Sue answered disbelievingly.

Billy and Danny ran full speed toward home. "Safe!" the umpire called after each boy slid into the bag.

Silver Creek won by two runs, and the team's cheering section broke into wide grins and loud whoops of joy. Susannah and Mary Sue congratulated each other as if their team had won a gold medal in the Olympics.

Down on the field the boys were pretty happy, too. They slapped each other on the back and elbowed their teammates good-naturedly. But Brett got them to calm down enough to line up and shake hands with the Pirates.

"Well, I about had a heart attack," Mary Sue confided. "I think these games take ten years off my life."

"I can see what you mean," Susannah conceded. "How often do they play?"

"Twice a week." She stood up. "I guess I'd better get down there. It was my turn to bring the refreshments."

"I'll help." Susannah followed the other woman to where the boys were milling around.

She was pleased to see that her suggestions for healthier snacks had filtered down even to this level. Mary Sue had cut up fresh oranges and baked a batch of Susannah's high fiber, high protein oatmeal-raisin cookies.

Brett came up behind Susannah, put his hands on her shoulders, and gave her a warm squeeze. Then he turned her around, and for several heartbeats his gaze focused on her lips.

She waited expectantly for his kiss, her body already slightly tingly, her mind already forgetting what she'd told him about public displays.

But apparently he remembered. There was a regretful look in his eyes as he let her go. He turned and eyed the cookies. "I assume those aren't forbidden."

"Not unless you've been bad," she answered lightly.

"If I were going to be bad, you'd have known it by now."

That was certainly the truth. It seemed that his willpower was stronger than hers.

"So what did you think of the game?" he asked.

"Your boys are terrific."

"And the coach?"

"Not bad."

"Not bad?" His blond eyebrows raised.

Just then, Billy came trotting over.

Brett turned to his son and ruffled his hair. "That was one heck of a steal you made there, sport."

"Aw, Dad." But it was obvious that the praise made him glow. "Since you're in such a good mood, I guess you won't mind me spending the night over at Danny's."

"So you want to leave your old dad at home again," Brett teased.

Billy gave them a sly look. "I'll bet you could talk Miss Lindsey into keeping you company."

"Maybe I can." Billy took a step back, and Brett put a hand on his shoulder. "Don't forget you're supposed to be helping me get that forty-footer in shape."

"I remember. I'll be home by ten."

"Nine."

"Nine-thirty."

"Okay," Brett agreed, and they shook on it.

Billy dashed off to catch up with his friend.

"He has a part-time job with you?" Susannah asked.

"Yes. That's the way he earns his spending money. But I make him put half his pay away in his college fund."

"Do you think he'll join you in the business when he grows up?" Susannah asked.

"I'd like that. But it will be up to him."

The conversation was interrupted when one of the players came up to Brett. "Where's the equipment bag?"

He pointed toward the bench. "Under there. Make sure all the bats and helmets are put away."

Brett supervised the cleanup. When most of the families had driven off, he walked back to where Susannah was picking up the orange peels and paper cups that hadn't landed in the trash can.

"Thanks for helping out."

"It's the least I could do after that exciting game." She hesitated and brushed the dust off her hands. He'd implied to Billy that they'd be doing something together that evening. But he hadn't really asked her.

"So, what do the health conscious grill instead of hamburgers and hot dogs?" he asked.

"Chicken. Fish. Turkey."

"How do you grill a turkey?"

"That's an advanced lesson."

"I suppose you have some recipes for the chicken and fish."

"Is this just idle curiosity? Or is the conversation leading up to something?"

"I was thinking during your radio program we could cook out this evening. But I wasn't sure what to cook."

"You were listening?"

"Yup. You were downright impressive, city lady."

Susannah was flattered that he'd listened, and she glowed in response to the praise.

"But I couldn't imagine strolling in the moonlight at fifteen minutes a mile!"

"I get the feeling you think of me as kind of a wet blanket."

"No; a challenge."

"I'm not sure that I like that better."

His lips tilted up in an irresistible grin. "Are you afraid to spend the evening at my place without a bunch of twelve-year-old chaperons?" he inquired.

"Of course not!"

"Good. Then it's a date. I'll go home and clean the grill."

"Let me bring the food."

"Fine. Why don't you come over around eight?"

Susannah agreed. Back home, she spent the next hour and a half getting ready. She had the urge to show Brett that her life-style didn't include having to make big sacrifices for the sake of good health.

After a quick trip to the grocery store, she marinated some chicken in a spicy teriyaki sauce. Then she made a pasta-and-vegetable salad. A fresh fruit bowl and speckled butter beans rounded out the menu.

On the short drive over to Brett's, she asked herself why it was important to prove anything to him. She could have told herself that he was a prominent citizen of Silver Creek whose support could make or break her program. But she wasn't fooling herself. She cared what he thought on a very personal level.

When she arrived, he was relaxing on the deck. He'd showered and shaved and replaced his uniform with crisp walking shorts and a jade-green cotton knit sweater that reminded her of the color of the water in the Caribbean.

"Looks like you've been busy," he observed, getting up to help her carry in the containers of food.

He'd been busy, too. The grill was sparkling clean, and the coals were white hot. A checkered cloth covered the patio table, which was set with two places. There was even a slender candle in a glass holder. She was surprised by the romantic touch.

"To keep the bugs away," he explained quickly when he saw her eyeing it.

While Susannah set out the dishes she'd prepared, Brett put the chicken on the grill. "Umm. Hope it tastes as good as it smells," he tossed over his shoulder. "How about a mint julep?"

That was stronger than her usual drink. But she was feeling a little daring tonight. "Sure," she agreed.

He brought out two tall, frosted glasses, each garnished with a large sprig of mint. They sat there sipping the drinks.

"There's been something I've wanted to ask you," Susannah said.

"Umm?"

"At the picnic, what was that little private exchange about fireworks?"

"You noticed." Brett leaned back in his chair. "That was just Donna's way of saying I told you so."

Susannah raised an eyebrow. "Am I missing something?"

"I was the head of the town Fourth of July Fireworks Committee."

"I haven't heard about any Fourth of July fireworks."

"That's right. The town council appropriated the money to hire a health consultant."

Susannah digested that information. "Oh. I see."

"Well, I have to admit you generate your own fireworks," Brett allowed.

Just then, lightning lit the night sky, and they grinned at each other.

"Are we going to get rained out?" Susannah asked.

"I think it'll hold off for a while."

Fifteen minutes later he brought the chicken to the table. As he took a bite, Susannah found herself waiting tensely for his verdict.

"This is really good." He sounded surprised.

Susannah shook her head.

"What?"

"You look positively shocked."

"Next you're going to have me eating quiche and liking it."

She laughed. "Don't bet on it. Quiche has too many eggs."

"Darn. And I'll just have to forget about that chocolate soufflé I was going to make."

"You don't look like the soufflé-type, either."

"Right. I'm just a simple country boy."

"Right."

Susannah found herself enjoying both the meal and the company. There was more to being with Brett than just that zing of awareness between them. The better she got to know the man, the more she liked him. He was a great storyteller and, unlike many people, he laughed just as hard when the joke was on him.

"One of the reasons why I know how to cope with Billy is that I remember some of the stunts I pulled when I was a kid," he told her.

"I bet you were a handful."

He grinned. "My mom always said if there was any justice in the world, I'd have a kid just like me." There was a reminiscent look on his face.

"I sense a good story coming on," Susannah prompted.

He tipped his chair back. "Well, you know how kids are. They hate school, and I was no exception. Especially when we had to do book reports. One time, back in third grade, my buddy and I came up with a real inventive way to get out of giving oral reports on Monday mornings."

"You put a thermometer on a light bulb so it would look like you had a fever?" she guessed.

"No. That would have been too tame. We wanted to be sure we'd be too bad off to go to school. So we scouted out this patch of poison ivy, took off our shirts and rubbed the stuff all over our chests and arms."

She looked at him in astonishment. "I guess third-graders aren't too smart."

"I've never been so miserable in my life. I found out I was super-allergic to the stuff. And I didn't get it just on my arms and chest. It was everywhere, including my rump. There was no comfortable way I could sit or lie or stand for weeks. It's kind of funny to remember it now, but believe me, it was pure hell at the time."

"I can imagine."

He leaned across the table toward her. "So tell me about the time you put the thermometer on the light bulb."

She flushed slightly. "It was the morning I was supposed to have a math test on long division. I always hated long division. Thank goodness for calculators. I never did learn to do it."

He laughed.

As they swapped more childhood memories and ate their dinner, the breeze picked up, and the lightning crept closer. Susannah could smell the rain in the air.

Just as they were finishing the last of the fruit salad, large drops started splattering the tablecloth.

Quickly they both gathered up the dishes and carried them into the house. Susannah had just started to rinse the plates when the storm broke around them with force.

Brett turned off the tap and captured her hands. "Leave that till later. We're going to miss the show."

"The show?"

Instead of answering, Brett led her to the wide screen porch on the other side of the house.

She looked at him questioningly.

"Haven't you ever gone out to watch a storm?"

"No. Isn't it dangerous?"

"Not if we stay on the porch."

Just then, the whole sky lit up with a jagged network of lightning. A moment later a loud crack of thunder sent Susannah shivering backward against Brett.

"Afraid of storms?" he asked.

"A little."

"Want to go back inside?"

She heard the disappointment in his voice and shook her head.

"We'll try it for a while." He pulled a wicker love seat back against the wall of the house, where it would be sheltered from the rain, and settled Susannah into the cushions. Then he sat down beside her.

Another crack of lightning was followed by a loud crash. Susannah flinched, and Brett slipped his arm around her. Wind lashed the porch, sending a spray of rain over them through the window screens. Susannah snuggled back against Brett and felt his arm tighten around her. Another crack of lightning made her jump.

"Okay?"

"Just a little wet."

They had both pitched their voices above the roar of the wind.

"Be glad we weren't out on the water when this hit."

"That's happened to you?"

"Of course. One of the worst storms I remember caught me on a sailboat three miles offshore."

It must have been dangerous, but she could tell from his voice that he found the experience exciting, too. "What was it like?"

"Winds strong enough to knock a man off the deck. Ten-foot-high waves. Man against nature."

She pictured him taking in sails as the rain and wind lashed his body. "You liked the challenge."

"I guess I did. But you don't think about that at the time; you're too busy trying to stay afloat."

His words put their present circumstance into perspective, but she still flinched when a lightning bolt hit nearby. "I always hated thunder and lightning when I was a kid," she confided.

"Did you hide under the bed?"

"Not quite. But if there was a storm in the middle of the night, I used to crawl under the covers at the end of my brother's bed. He'd wake up in the morning and find me tangled in his feet."

Brett laughed. "I wouldn't mind waking up in the morning like that."

"Well, I'm a big girl now. I don't do that anymore."

"Shucks."

The wind shifted, sending a spray of rain in their direction. Brett pulled her head against his chest and planted a kiss on her damp hair.

"You get to me, city lady," he murmured.

"I'm not trying to."

"I'd hate to imagine the effect if you were trying." He shifted her around and looked down into her face. She'd braided her hair again for the evening. Now he reached around and found the band that held it fast. He slipped it off and then slowly began to unbraid the silky strands.

It was a very intimate gesture, and she felt as if she should tell him to stop. But she was powerless to speak as his hands combed through her hair, fanning out the tresses and arranging them in a dark curtain around her shoulders.

"It's cute when it's braided, but it's sexy when it's down like this," he murmured.

Her eyes fluttered closed, and her lips parted for his kiss. His lips covered hers with only a whisper of pressure. They hovered together on the edge of their own private storm.

But the tempest never broke. Instead of deepening the kiss and folding her into his arms, he pulled away from her.

Susannah's eyes snapped open, and she stared up at him, confused and disoriented.

Desire warred with conscience inside Brett. He drew in a steadying breath. He knew beyond doubt that he could sweep Susannah along with him to the place where passion raged. But no matter how much he wanted her, he didn't want their lovemaking to be that way. He wanted a conscious decision on her part that this was the right thing for the two of them to do.

"If things go any further now, it's going to be damn hard to stop." His voice was husky, and there was an implied question at the end of his sentence.

It was at that moment that Susannah realized she was falling in love with Brett. The urge to take him in her arms and just let herself respond to him was almost overwhelming. She'd never felt like this about anybody before. And there was an element of fear mixed in with the rush of pleasure that threatened to blot out rational thought.

She didn't know how to answer him. She only knew that being in his arms made her lose control. And she was afraid of that.

"The rain's stopped." She made an effort to focus on the surroundings rather than the man beside her.

"But it's probably going to start again. If you don't want to end up staying here all night, you'd better go while you can."

Susannah nodded and stood up. She quickly pulled her hair back into a ponytail. Brett watched, but didn't say anything more.

Before she could change her mind, she retrieved her purse from the front hall and left. Now that the rain had stopped, mist lay thickly on the driveway. She turned, wondering if she should go back. But the mist had closed off everything behind her. It was as though Brett's house had totally vanished.

She had to fight off a feeling of emptiness as she climbed into her car. Why was she fleeing from happiness?

Probably because she didn't think it could last. All the objections she'd thought of before still stood. Brett was only thinking of this as temporary. He had even reminded his son that she wasn't going to be in town after the summer.

Was there any way she could make it more than that? Susannah thought about Silver Creek. She liked the relaxed life-style. But she couldn't picture herself being content to teach a few exercise classes for the rest of her life. Her career meant something to her. It was deeply satisfying. There was no way she could simply give it up.

The road took a sharp turn to the right. But because of the fog, she didn't see it until the last minute. She slammed on her brakes, and the car teetered at the edge of a ditch. Her heart was pounding against her rib cage as she backed up. She'd better pay attention to her driving if she wanted to get home in one piece.

After that, she drove more slowly. But she couldn't stop thinking about the dilemma. She didn't want to give up her career, yet the thought of not seeing Brett anymore made tears gather in her eyes.

What was wrong with enjoying whatever they could have together for the summer? she asked herself. She couldn't think of a reason. If the fog hadn't been so treacherous, she might have turned around and driven back to his house.

It had taken her twice as long as it should have to get home. As she climbed the steps, she heard the phone ringing. It didn't stop as she hurried across the living room. "Hello?"

"Thank God you're okay." It was Brett. "If I'd known how bad it was outside, I never would have let you leave."

Her hand tightened on the receiver. "I'm fine." Before she could stop herself she added, "I thought about turning around and coming back."

"Because of the fog?"

"No. Because of you."

She heard him draw in his breath. "What's that supposed to mean?"

Susannah cleared her throat. "You said I was getting to you. Well, you're getting to me, too."

"Now's a hell of a time to tell me that."

She laughed. "I know."

"I could be over there in fifteen minutes."

"It's not safe to drive. You might end up in a ditch. I almost did."

She heard him mutter an expletive.

"Don't get upset. I'm all right."

"So what happens now?"

She hesitated for a moment. "Do you want to have dinner over here tomorrow?"

There was no hesitation in his reply. "Yes."

She had a sudden attack of cold feet. What exactly was she inviting him over for? "You could bring Billy."

He laughed. "I thought from the drift of the conversation that we were beyond the chaperon stage."

"But what's he going to eat if you leave him home?"

"Fish. As it happens, Joe's father is taking him and a couple of other guys out on the river for a few days."

"Oh?"

"So you don't have to worry about that."

"Brett, do you really think we can keep seeing each other—without it getting all over town?"

"I've managed it before."

"Oh."

He didn't volunteer any more details. "What time do you want me?" he asked instead.

"Uh—"

"Let's make it early," he suggested. "What about five?"

"I guess."

"Don't fix dessert. I'll bring something."

Susannah wondered what that was going to be.

They talked for a few minutes more. "I've got an early day tomorrow, so I'd better turn in," Brett finally said.

"All right."

"I wish I could say good-night to you properly."

"How's that?" she managed.

His laugh was rich and sexy. "I guess you'll have to wait until tomorrow to find out."

Chapter Seven

Susannah had a lot of things to do the next day, including a grocery-store cooking demonstration. It was an effort to keep her thoughts on making low-fat fruit pancakes and answering questions about oat bran.

When it was finally over, Paul, the store manager, greeted her as a celebrity, telling her that sales of fresh produce were up twenty percent since she'd started the demonstrations. "I'm even selling tons of brussels sprouts. That must have been some recipe you gave out on the radio yesterday."

Susannah smiled and nodded. She was interested in the town's progress, but right now she really wanted to think about her own menu for the evening. Tonight was the first time she'd have Brett over.

Paul finally left her, and she stood in the produce section debating whether to get fresh zucchini or green beans. Finally she got a pound of the former and an eggplant so she could make a ratatouille. To go with it, she bought red snapper, which she decided to bake with an herb stuffing. A crisp tossed salad would round out the meal.

The phone was ringing when she arrived back at the cottage. Balancing her bag of groceries, she tried to find the key in her pocketbook. Mayor Rollins had told her that she didn't need to lock the door, but she couldn't break the habit of a lifetime in a couple of weeks.

By the time she got inside and picked up, she wished she'd taken his advice—there was only a dial tone on the other end of the line. Had Brett called to check about this evening? If so, he'd call back. But the phone didn't ring again during the rest of the afternoon while she prepared dinner.

Living alone, Susannah didn't often go to the trouble of fixing a fancy meal. But she loved to cook. This afternoon she stood at the sink in the small kitchen, humming as she washed and cut up the vegetables.

By the time the doorbell rang at five after five, Susannah had everything under control. She'd taken a shower and changed into a mint-green sundress. She stood before the mirror, trying several hairstyles. Brett had told her that her hair looked sexy down, and she wanted to please him. Yet her conservative side didn't want to announce quite that much. So she finally settled on a compromise that made her grin. The front was pulled back and held with a clip. The back was very loose.

When she opened the door, she felt her breath catch in her throat. Brett looked devastatingly masculine in dark slacks and a sea-blue shirt that matched his eyes.

He stared at her for a moment. "You look beautiful."

"So do you."

He grinned. "Thanks." He held out a cone of white paper.

Susannah accepted it and looked inside to find a bouquet of mixed blue and white daisies. "I didn't expect you to be so romantic."

"Neither did I. You just kind of bring it out in me." He paused. "I wonder if it's a reaction to all that health food you're feeding me."

She laughed and stepped aside to let him in. "I doubt it."

"I've got something else in the car. I'll be right back."

Susannah was at the sink, arranging the flowers in a vase, when he came back in carrying a half-bushel basket. It was filled with beautifully ripe peaches.

"I haven't seen those in the store yet."

"One of my customers brought them up from south Georgia." He had a slightly wistful look on his face.

"What?"

"I was thinking. We've been eating all these healthy meals. Do you think we could reward ourselves with some, uh, homemade pie."

"Oh, so you had an ulterior motive."

"I do love peach pie."

"What if I make you something just as good that's a lot better for you."

"That I have to taste."

"You can slice about five cups of peaches while I make a topping."

"It's a deal."

Brett was a lot better with the peaches than he had been with the carrots. Maybe because she handed him the right knife. By the time he'd finished his assignment, Susannah had made a brown-sugar-and-flour topping.

As she began to sprinkle it over the fruit in a baking dish, Brett came up behind her and put his arms around her waist.

"That sure looks easier than making a pie crust," he observed as he pulled her close.

For a moment she leaned back against him. Then he bent to brush his lips behind her right ear. "Have any other cooking techniques you want to share?" he murmured.

"You're making it hard for me to think about what to do next."

His lips nuzzled her neck. "I assume you put it in the oven."

"Right." She half turned and looked at him. A little knot of tension twisted in her stomach. This wasn't quite how she'd pictured starting off the evening. "Do you want to eat dinner or not?"

"I'm thinking."

"Well, I spent all afternoon fixing it."

"In that case, let's eat."

Susannah was still feeling a bit jittery as she set the flowers in the middle of the glass-topped table on the screened porch. "Have a seat, and I'll serve the salad," she told Brett.

When she joined him at the table, he reached out and covered her hand with his. "I get the feeling having me over to dinner alone is making you a little bit nervous, city lady."

"Who, me?"

He grinned at her. "I'll behave myself—as long as you want me to."

"Thanks."

There was a wry smile on his face as he helped himself to salad.

"What are you thinking about?"

"About the first time I had dinner alone with a woman. I told my parents I was spending the night with my friend Charlie. But I was really at Sally Fitzgerald's house. Her parents were away for the evening."

"You spent the night at Sally Fitzgerald's? Are you sure this is a G-rated story?"

"PG 13. Actually, I was sixteen. She grilled hot dogs for dinner. But we didn't have more than an hour together after eating."

"What happened?"

"I'd been planning the big event for two or three weeks and had everything set. Nothing could go wrong. But Charlie didn't know his father was having a poker game and that my dad was invited. When he asked to speak to me about something, Charlie told him I was in the bathroom and rushed upstairs to call me at Sally's."

"And?"

"That was the fastest half-mile I ever ran. I got thorns in my hands climbing up the trellis to Charlie's second floor bathroom."

"And what did Sally think about all that?"

"I don't know. I was too embarrassed to speak to her again."

"And you should have been—taking advantage of a poor girl while her parents were out of town."

Brett helped himself to the main dish. "Honey, it was her idea."

"And you want to make sure I understand what a prize I'm getting?"

His rich laugh made her skin tingle. But strangely enough, she also began to relax. By the time she served the peach crisp, they were on very comfortable terms.

He took a bite of the dessert and rolled his eyes. "The rest of the dinner was wonderful, but this is heavenly. Are you sure it isn't fattening?"

"I wouldn't serve it every day if I were trying to lose weight. But it's more nutritious than peach pie—less fat and sugar and no salt."

"In that case, I'll have a second helping." He took another small serving and forked up an appreciative bite. "You'd make someone a fine wife," he said, and then paused, realizing what had just come out of his mouth.

For a moment they stared at each other.

"So how come a woman like you isn't married?" Brett suddenly asked.

Susannah dabbed at her lips with her napkin. She could just say something frivolous, but she sensed more than just casual interest behind the question.

"I got involved with my career, and somehow the guys I dated just didn't seem like husband material." Before Brett could inquire as to what she considered "husband material," she asked her own leading question. "It must have been pretty hard raising Billy by yourself. Why didn't *you* remarry?"

A melancholy look crossed his face. "I had a really good marriage," he said slowly, setting down his fork. "And I didn't want to settle for second-best just to have a woman around to help take care of my son." He gave her a direct look. "I sort of gave up thinking about it until recently."

She felt herself go warm inside.

Brett stood up. "Come on. It's only fair for me to help you clean up."

He'd put an end to the revealing conversation, and Susannah, not exactly sure how far she wanted to pursue the topic right now, decided it best to follow his lead.

While they worked, Brett tuned in a local country-rock station. The kind of music the Rockabillies had played at the welcoming supper filled the kitchen.

He washed dishes and handed them to Susannah for drying, humming along with the lead singers.

"Your secret fantasy is to be a country-western star," she guessed.

"Not even close." His eyes were filled with lazy sensuality as he handed her the last glass. "I've been thinking about that first night when we danced. Dance with me now."

"Here? In the kitchen?"

"If you don't like the kitchen, come on out on the porch."

"But we're alone," she protested.

"That makes it all the nicer."

His large hand closed around her smaller one, and she felt a tingle of anticipation tease her nerve endings.

They went outside. The sun was low over the river, turning the water to liquid fire and the sky to a warm glow. Brett turned to face her and then put her hands up on his shoulders before clasping her around the waist. At first neither of them moved. Then, as if they both suddenly remembered what they were supposed to be doing, they began to sway to the music.

"You're so naturally graceful. But, then, I liked the way you moved even before I met you," he confided.

"From that tape?"

"Umm-hmm. Has anyone ever told you what a turn-on your terrific body is." For emphasis he slid his hands down the length of her back to her hips.

"Is that what you like about me—my body?" she teased.

"Not just that." His lips nibbled at her earlobe. "I like your sense of humor. Your spunk. Almost everything about you."

She angled her head back so that she could meet his eyes. "Almost? What is it you don't like?"

He hesitated.

"Come on. I can take it."

"Well, you're pretty stubborn. And you tend to want to get your own way."

"Oh, I do?" She stopped swaying to the music and considered that for a moment. "You may be right. But I'd say it takes one to know one, Tanner!"

His laugh vibrated against her cheek. "Let's hope we both get our way tonight."

They kissed—a long, sweet exploration of each other's mouths. She could taste the lingering cinnamon spice from the dessert on his lips. Could he taste it on hers?

"You know, when I first met you, I was set on resisting you," he finally murmured in a husky voice.

"Oh, but you hid it so well."

He gave her a little nip on the ear. "There are some things a man can't hide," he whispered softly, and tightened his hold around her waist.

She didn't have to ask what he meant—she could feel the hard muscle of his legs and thighs pressing into her. If they'd been dancing this way in public, every head would have turned in their direction, Susannah thought.

But they didn't have an audience to worry about tonight.

Instead, she could concentrate on the feel of Brett's sun-streaked hair beneath her fingertips, the ocean-fresh smell of his after-shave and the delicious tingle of excitement going through her as his hands began to trace random patterns on her back.

The song ended, and the announcer went into a commercial. Brett stopped dancing but didn't let Susannah go. "Thank you," she said. "That was—"

"Better than peach pie. But this will be even yummier." Slowly, his hands threaded through her hair to the back of her neck and tilted her face back up to his. As her lips melted against his, Brett's fingers slipped under the thin straps of her sundress, working them inch by inch off her shoulders. Susannah shivered in his arms. Then his lips were feathering down her neck and nuzzling the exposed skin. She could feel the caress all the way to her toes, and her heart was thudding so loudly in her chest that she was sure Brett could hear it.

Suddenly she realized that the thudding was coming from the other room. Someone was beating on the front door. She twisted out of Brett's arms and tried to catch her breath. Hastily, she pulled up the straps of her dress and patted her hair into place.

"Whoever it is, tell 'em to come back tomorrow," he suggested.

Susannah was tempted to do just that. But her eyes widened in surprise when she opened the door and saw three men on her front porch, one of whom she recognized. "Jack! What are *you* doing here?"

"Now is that any way to greet your boss?" Jack chastised. "The boys from Cable News and I drove all the way from Atlanta just to cover your Silver Creek activities. I'd like you to meet Ralph Cantrell and Luke Martin from the *Life-styles* program. They want to do several segments for next week's shows."

Susannah knew she should offer her hand politely to the jeans-and-T-shirt-clad young men. Instead she stared openmouthed at Jack. "But we agreed—" she finally managed.

"Tried to phone you, but I didn't get an answer."

So that was who had been calling when she came in with the groceries.

"Listen, you can't . . . I don't want—"

"Don't worry. We'll work it all out."

Somehow Susannah doubted it. She could just imagine what Brett would think about this. Ohmygosh, she thought. He was right on the back porch.

"How about fixing us a cool drink, and we can work out the schedule?" Jack said. "Which way is the bathroom?"

"Down the hall and to the right," Susannah muttered, trying to think. Jack pulled the screen door open and walked right into the house. Susannah followed on his heels.

"Did you get rid of them, honey?" Brett called out from the back of the house.

"I didn't know you had company," Jack remarked. "Bad time?"

"It's going to get worse," Susannah predicted as Brett sauntered into the hall.

"There's some iced tea in the refrigerator and clean glasses over the sink. You and Luke just go in and help yourself," she told the men from Cable News. They seemed glad to get out of the crowded hall.

Brett and Jack were taking stock of each other like two tomcats who'd suddenly met in a dark alley.

"Brett Tanner, president of the Chamber of Commerce, meet Jack Thompson, vice president of Healthways." Susannah made the introductions and hoped for the best.

"Oh, hey, glad I ran into you here. You're probably just the guy to help us make the most of this publicity opportunity."

Brett crossed his arms and leaned against the wall, looking deceptively at ease.

Susannah felt her stomach clench. "Jack, I don't think—"

"No. No. I'm just itching to hear what y'all have been cooking up."

"Brett, this wasn't my idea. I haven't—"

Before Susannah could finish her protest, Jack enthusiastically launched into a catalog of the national attention he had in store for Silver Creek. "I figured we'd start by interviewing residents who are getting some benefits out of Susannah's program. And, of course, we'll showcase the local businesses that are sponsors. What do you think?" He was so wound up that he didn't see Brett's eyes narrow and his expression harden from wary to cynical.

Brett looked from Jack to Susannah. "I think you've got a lot of nerve to come in here and exploit us. The people of this town thought they were hiring a health consultant. They didn't bargain on having Silver Creek turned into a media circus for the benefit of your company's public image."

Susannah hadn't been particularly happy with Jack's methods, but Brett's accusations were way out of proportion. She found herself jumping in defensively. "Now just a second—"

Brett gave her a look that would have frozen a blast furnace. "I'm sure you and Jack have a lot to talk about," he cut her off. "So I'll just leave you to it." With that, he opened the front door and stepped out.

"I didn't plan this!" she shouted after him.

"And pigs can fly." He slammed the door behind him.

"What's with that guy?" Jack asked. "You'd think he'd be tickled to get some national publicity for this burg."

"I'm afraid Brett doesn't see it that way. Frankly, I wish you hadn't gone ahead with this on your own."

"It was now or never."

"I guess it would look pretty bad if I tried to send the film crew away."

"Baby, you can bet they'd think you had something to hide. Then they'd really be all over this place."

Susannah sighed. "Let me at least warn the mayor what's up. Then I guess we'd better start discussing what would make good footage."

Susannah felt a little better after talking to Dwayne Rollins. He saw the arrival of the film crew as a way of countering the bad publicity that had prompted the fitness program in the first place, and as a golden opportunity to promote Silver Creek's tourist industry.

"Let me get in touch with Bonnie," he said excitedly. "She's the one who's been keeping a record of the total number of people who've signed up."

When she hung up, Susannah got out a notebook and pencil. She didn't like Jack's methods but, as an instructor, she was very aware of how good publicity could be used as a motivator. Maybe this was just what she needed to add some excitement.

Susannah, Jack and the film crew spent the next few hours making plans. The next day they checked out possible location shots. When they finally quit around five in the afternoon, she was exhausted. She wanted to flop into bed for a short nap before her eight-o'clock cooking class.

But she kept remembering the angry look on Brett's face when he'd stormed out last night. Before the crew started to film, she wanted to try to make him see why this wasn't such a bad thing for Silver Creek. So she climbed into her car and started out for the marina.

She was thinking about what she wanted to say as much as she was watching the road when a black-and-silver racing bike streaked out from a side lane almost directly in front of her. Her heart leapt into her throat as she slammed on the brakes. Swerving, she just managed to avoid the rider. But the near miss caused him to lose his balance. She watched in alarm as he skidded into the ditch at the side of the road.

Susannah scrambled out of the car and ran toward the rider. It wasn't until she reached his side that she realized it was Billy Tanner.

She squatted down beside him and put her hand on his shoulder. "Billy, honey, are you all right?"

He sat up, looking dazed and embarrassed.

"Are you hurt?" Susannah repeated.

"I don't think so. Gee, Miss Lindsey, I'm sorry, I forgot to look when I crossed the road."

Susannah gave him a careful inspection. The edge of his jams was frayed, and there was a nasty abrasion on one of his knees. "We'd better get you home and cleaned up."

He looked at her pleadingly, tears glistening in the corners of his eyes. "Please, don't tell Dad what I did. He'll ground me."

"It might be hard to keep this a secret. But let's worry about getting you fixed up first."

"Is my bike busted?"

"The rim of your front wheel is bent. I think that's all. Come on, I'll take you home now."

She helped him hobble to the car. Then she put the bike in the trunk.

They drove the short distance in silence, with Billy casting her sideways glances. "I don't think Dad will be home till later," the boy confided when they turned into the driveway and she cut the engine. "I hope he's in a better mood this afternoon than he was this morning."

Susannah closed her eyes for a moment. She hoped he was in a better mood, too.

Inside, she sat Billy down on the edge of the bathtub. After handing him a cloth to wipe his face, she gently washed his injury. The skin was raw. "I remember getting scrapes like this when I was a kid. You're going to have to be careful when you slide into second base," she said.

While he was still smiling weakly, she applied hydrogen peroxide. He winced but took it silently. Then Susannah taped a sterile gauze pad over his knee. On impulse, she sat down beside him on the edge of the tub and put her arm around him. To her surprise, he leaned against her. "Thanks," he whispered.

"That's okay. If you weren't so grown-up, I'd offer to kiss it and make it better. My mom used to do that when I was little."

He twisted the washcloth in his hand. "So did my mom. Dad's really great, but sometimes I miss her."

She nodded, not sure what to say next. No matter how caring Brett was, he couldn't completely be both mother and father to his son.

Billy looked down at his knee. "If you didn't go so heavy on the vegetable stuff, I'll bet you'd be a good mom."

The comment startled her. In the back of her mind, she'd thought about the time when she might have a family of her own. But she'd never really met anyone she wanted to settle down with—until she'd met Brett.

"Did you and my dad have a fight?" Billy asked suddenly.

Susannah looked at him and then quickly down at her hands. It was strange how his thoughts were running along the same track as hers. "Not exactly a fight. More of a misunderstanding," she murmured. "I was hoping to talk to him about it."

Billy nodded. "I always wait until after dinner. He ain't as stubborn when he's full."

Susannah grinned. That certainly fit in with her own experience, right from their first meeting at the VFW hall. "Thanks for the tip."

They looked at each other knowingly. But the mood was broken the next moment when they heard the door slam.

"Billy?"

"In the bathroom, Dad."

Susannah found herself clutching the bottle of antiseptic. She looked up to see Brett's large form filling the doorway.

"What's going on?" he demanded.

"Billy had an accident on his bike. I brought him home."

He turned immediately to the boy. "Are you hurt, son?"

"Naw. Scraped my knee. Miss Lindsey fixed it up. See." He raised his leg slightly and flinched.

"Take it easy," Brett advised.

"I'm okay." To prove the point, he stood up. Then, after glancing from one adult to the other, he ducked under his dad's arm and headed for his bedroom. Susannah heard the door close.

Susannah stared up at Brett.

"How did you happen to run into Billy?" he inquired.

"I was on my way over to talk to you."

"We don't have anything to talk about."

"Yes, we do."

He leaned against the doorjamb. "Okay, shoot."

Suddenly it felt very crowded in the small room. And craning her neck up to look at the man taking up most of the space was putting her at a disadvantage. "Do we have to have this conversation in the bathroom?"

Brett shrugged and turned. Susannah followed him down the hall to the family room. Instead of sitting on one of the couches, he remained standing.

Susannah pressed her hands against her sides. "Brett, I know what you were thinking yesterday."

He raised a questioning eyebrow.

"You wouldn't listen to me last night. I know you think I arranged for Jack to bring that film crew to town. Well, I didn't."

"You expect me to believe that he'd come here without even mentioning it to you?"

"Okay, we did discuss it. But I told him I wasn't sure about the idea and wanted to clear it with the town council first."

"But you didn't," Brett pointed out.

She swallowed. "I didn't have a chance to."

"Maybe you weren't very forceful in discouraging Jack," he said in a level voice that was maddening because of the control he was exercising.

In response, Susannah heard her own tone grow strident. "For crying out loud, he's my boss. I can't exactly tell him his publicity ideas stink."

"And now that they're here, you're not going to miss the opportunity to get on national TV."

"Brett Tanner, that's not the point. You've got this one little idea stuck in your head that we're here to rip off Silver Creek. *It's just not true.* For your information, Dwayne Rollins and a lot of other people are getting really excited about being on national TV."

"Well, whoopee for them."

Susannah rarely lost her temper, but right now she felt like grabbing Brett's broad shoulders and shaking some sense into him. She knew it wouldn't do any good, so instead she flapped her arms in aggravation and headed toward the door. Before stepping out, she turned and gave him a measured look. "You know, you're the most pigheaded man I ever met."

"It just takes a certain kind of woman to bring it out in me," he shot back.

"Happy to oblige."

They stood regarding each other for another moment. Then she pushed the screen door open.

"Wait a minute," he called out.

A hint of softness in the request made her heart leap, and she turned to face him again. "What?"

"I, uh, didn't thank you for taking care of Billy," he said grudgingly.

"Don't mention it." Without another word she turned and left.

The heated exchange left her more determined than ever to make the publicity experience a good one for Silver Creek as well as Healthways.

Over the next few days Susannah was delighted to see how many of the townspeople wanted to tell their stories on TV.

That was lucky, because no one could turn around without stepping on the Cable News crew. They filmed an exercise class and a cooking demonstration, watched Donna Nevins prepare supper and even invaded Laura Henderson's pottery studio to hear her explain how much more energy she had since she'd dropped fifteen pounds.

Each evening, a five-minute segment about the town was broadcast. Residents were constantly coming up to Susannah with excited accounts of seeing themselves on TV. By the end of the week merchants began reporting that media attention had brought an influx of visitors to town.

There was almost a party atmosphere about the whole week that would have put Susannah in a great mood. Except that the only person conspicuously absent from the activities was Brett. She told herself that she didn't want him there. He'd only spoil the fun. Then why did her eyes search every crowded room for his sun-streaked hair?

For so many years she'd felt in control of her life. She had a great job, friends, an apartment she loved. Why was one man suddenly so important?

He wasn't, she told herself firmly. And besides, this was probably the best thing that could have happened, anyway. She was going to be leaving Silver Creek. Now that she'd made a clean break with Brett, they wouldn't have to agonize over saying goodbye to each other.

It all made perfect sense. But the rationalizations didn't really make her feel any better.

The film crew left on Friday. By Monday morning things had settled down, and the town was almost back to normal again. But Susannah's eight a.m. exercise class was still talking about the thrill of being celebrities.

"You know," Laura said, "I used to eat doughnuts when I was nervous. The day before they came out to film at my studio, I went through two bags of carrots, a bunch of celery and three red peppers."

"It's great you stuck to the diet under that kind of pressure. You've got a lot of willpower, Laura. And you're really going to wow them at your reunion," Susannah said approvingly.

The dark-haired young woman nodded. "And that's not all. A gallery owner in Charleston saw my stoneware on TV. He's coming up here to have a look at it."

"That's wonderful!" Donna said.

"A bunch of us are going out to celebrate our progress," Laura continued. "Want to come?"

"Where are you going?" Susannah asked.

A silly smile played at the corners of Laura's lips. "We used to go out for pizza. Now we go to bingo night at the First Baptist Church. It's a lot of fun. Really."

"Say yes," Donna urged. Mary Sue and Jeanette also voiced their encouragement.

Susannah laughed. "Sure."

Laura offered to pick her up, and at eight o'clock that night, Susannah found herself in a bingo hall already crowded with an interesting mix of players from teenagers all the way up to senior citizens. Electric fans in the ceiling stirred the warm air. Some of the crowd had brought along hand-held paddle-shaped fans. On the back of each was an advertisement for Walker's Funeral Home.

Donna, Mary Sue and Jeanette were already settled at a table near the board where the numbers were put up as they were called. The women had saved two seats, which Susannah and Laura promptly claimed. Glancing around, Susannah noticed that some of the women had a bunch of bingo cards. Still, she decided to start with just one. Then she learned that in addition to cash, there were mystery prizes donated by members of the business community.

The women were in a relaxed mood. Between rounds they sipped diet soft drinks and nibbled on the unsalted popcorn Laura had brought.

"This is the one night a week I leave my kids with my husband, and get out for a little R and R," Jeanette said.

"Not all men are that accommodatin'," Donna observed.

"You can say that again."

That brought a knowing laugh from everyone.

Mary Sue cast Susannah a sidelong glance. "At least they treat you nicer when you're still courtin'."

Susannah felt her cheeks heat. "We're *not* courting."

There were some eyebrows raised.

"In fact, we're not even talking to each other."

All eyes were riveted on her. Susannah wished she'd kept her mouth shut.

"Oh, that's a shame. You and Brett made such a good couple," Mary Sue murmured.

Laura tried to change the subject. "Wasn't it exciting about the way the film crew was all over town?"

"Everywhere except the marina," Donna chimed in. "I hear Brett kicked them off his property."

Jack had forgotten to tell Susannah about that. But she wasn't surprised. She also wasn't surprised that the conversation had come back to her least favorite topic.

"He's one stubborn cuss when he digs his heels in," Mary Sue said.

"Oh, they all are," Donna pronounced.

"The way to get around them is to build up their egos," Jeanette put in.

If Brett's ego was any bigger, he probably couldn't pull a polo shirt over his head, Susannah thought. But she kept that to herself.

She looked up to see Laura listening with interest. Of the group, they were the only two who were single.

"Yeah. It's all psychology," Mary Sue agreed. "When I want Burt to fix something around the house, I get out his tool kit and start waving the screwdriver like I'm going to fix it myself. He always comes barging in and takes over before I can do any damage!"

The group laughed.

Susannah was relieved when a new game started, and the talk of men in general, and Brett in specific, stopped. But even as she tried to listen to the numbers being called, she was thinking about how things had gone so wrong between her and Brett. And she wasn't sure Mary Sue's advice would have helped.

"B5," the announcer called out.

Susannah was hardly paying attention.

Laura nudged her. "Wake up, you've got that." She leaned over and put the marker on the correct square. "Hey, you've won!"

Susannah looked down at her card. To her astonishment, one column was completely filled in. "Bingo!" she exclaimed, then called her numbers back to the announcer. They were all on the board.

"Come on down, little lady, and claim your prize."

Susannah knew she was grinning as she walked to the front of the room. She hadn't expected anything like this tonight.

"You've won a mystery prize worth a hundred dollars," the man told her as he handed her an envelope.

Susannah tore it open and pulled out a white card.

"What is it?" Donna called out.

"It's—it's a free charter fishing trip from Tanner's Marina."

The crowd cheered its approval.

With a forced smile plastered on her face, Susannah moved back down the aisle to her seat. The first thing she'd ever won in her life, and she knew she wasn't going to collect.

Chapter Eight

Two days later Susannah was working on the notes for her radio program when the phone rang. "Hello?"

"Hi."

She almost dropped the receiver. The deep, masculine voice on the other end of the line belonged to Brett.

"Are you still there?" he inquired.

"Umm-hmm," she answered cautiously. Was he phoning to chew her out about something else she'd done?

"I guess you're wondering why I'm calling," he continued.

"Umm-hmm."

"I, uh, heard about that fantastic prize you won the other night at the bingo game."

Susannah rolled her eyes toward the ceiling. There was hardly anything you could keep secret in Silver Creek. Probably all his fishing buddies had called Brett to tell him the good news. She wouldn't have put it past

Laura or one of the other women to have given him an anonymous tip.

"Oh?" she responded noncommittally.

"Aren't you planning to collect?"

"You told me once you didn't think I'm the fishing type."

"I've been wrong before."

"Brett, what's going on? The last time we talked, you made it pretty clear that you wouldn't go out of your way to give me the time of day."

"I might have been a bit hasty."

"A bit?"

"Oh, all right. I was a jackass."

Susannah laughed. Now that the tension had been broken, she suddenly realized just how uptight she'd been since she'd last seen him. "You were. But I didn't expect you to admit it."

He cleared his throat. "I was at the meeting of the Chamber of Commerce late last week. Everybody was thrilled with the publicity from those special reports."

"Everyone but you."

"Well, I did get a number of new customers who heard about Silver Creek on the evening news."

She could have rubbed that in his face. Instead she said, "I'm glad."

"I've missed you."

The plaintive note in his voice brought a lump to her throat. "I'm glad about that, too."

"You could have said you missed me."

"Maybe I did—a little."

"So accept my apology and come fishing with me on Friday."

"I have a lot to do."

"We both know you don't have any exercise classes. And you deserve some time off for good behavior."

She thought about it. "If I work hard all morning, I could be free by lunch."

"Then I'll take care of the food. Change into something comfortable and tennis shoes and come on out to the marina whenever you're done."

"It's a deal."

Well, so much for the advice she'd given herself earlier in the week, she reflected as she hung up. She felt ridiculously happy as she sat staring into space, thinking about seeing Brett again. She was like a teenage girl before her first date. Realizing she could easily spend the rest of the day musing on Friday's meeting, she buckled down to work.

Susannah found that the perfect way to channel her excess energy was to choreograph a new routine for her advanced exercise class. She picked a tape of fifties music and started working out an intricate set of moves. It had to be fun and still provide the necessary aerobic benefits. An hour and a half later she was pleased with the results—and ready for the shower.

But after she'd changed into a cotton nightdress and climbed into bed, she couldn't stop thinking about Brett. It wouldn't take much encouragement for her to fall all over the man. One of his lazy smiles was enough to make her start to quiver. One of his kisses made her as giddy as if she'd drunk a bottle of champagne.

Well, now that she'd had a little time to step away from the relationship, she wasn't sure she liked feeling that way. And she certainly wasn't going to give Brett the impression that she was ready to take up where they'd left off before Jack had knocked on the door.

She was going to play it cool. After all, this wasn't really a date. She was just collecting a bingo prize.

Despite her resolve, her stomach was fluttering two days later as she pulled into a vacant parking space at the marina. She'd heard a lot about the place, but she'd never actually been there. She glanced around with interest. It was a beautiful setting with the sun-sparkled water, the acres of sailboats and cabin cruisers tied up along piers. The whole operation was bigger than she'd imagined. In addition to the office, Susannah could see a grocery and general store, a carryout restaurant and a bustling dry-dock.

In the office, she asked the middle-aged secretary to let Brett know she'd arrived. He came striding out of a back room, looking pleased to see her.

Susannah hadn't realized how much she'd missed him until she took in his windblown hair, warm blue eyes and easy smile.

"I'm glad you could make it." He reached out, took both her hands and squeezed them fondly. "You look wonderful." Instead of letting go, he continued to hold on to her as if he couldn't bear to break the contact now that they were together again.

And she felt the same way. She hadn't seen him, hadn't touched him in over a week. She'd forgotten the little zing that even this closeness generated. A voice from some tiny corner of her brain tried to remind her that she'd come here simply to collect a prize.

The secretary cleared her throat. "If you're not back by five, I'll just lock up."

Brett dropped Susannah's hands and whirled around. "Uh, fine. Maybe we'd better go pick up lunch."

In tacit agreement, they stayed a few feet apart as they walked down the dock and into the restaurant.

"I would have asked the cook, Jimmy Bob, to fix something hot, but he doesn't know how to do anything that isn't greasy," Brett explained.

"Want me to give him some tips?"

"He's too old and crotchety." Brett took a wicker basket out of the walk-in refrigerator and then led the way to a small but nicely appointed cabin cruiser. Across the stern were the words *Risky Venture*.

Susannah raised an eyebrow. "I hope the name doesn't refer to lack of seaworthiness."

Brett laughed. "No. She handles like a dream. This is the first boat I bought when I came back home. The name refers to the way I felt about leaving a steady job and cashing in every share of stock I owned so I could open my own business."

Susannah looked at him with new respect. She hadn't realized what a risk Brett had taken in starting all over again back in Silver Creek. "Well, it really looks as if you've made it work," she murmured.

"I'm feeling good about it." He turned and glanced over his shoulder at the sun, which was still high overhead. "Enough about me. We've got a date with some largemouth bass." He stretched out his hand. Susannah took it, and he helped her down into the boat. Then he cast off the ropes and jumped down onto the deck beside her. The boat rocked, and she sat down abruptly on one of the cushioned benches that lined the cockpit.

"Make yourself comfortable," he said.

"I think I already have."

After stowing the picnic basket, Brett started the engine and eased the small cruiser out into the channel. As soon as *Risky Venture* was clear of the congested area, he opened the throttle, making the cruiser go faster.

"Where are we going?" Susannah asked above the noise of the engine.

"Upriver. There's a spot I know where the fish stand in line for the privilege of gettin' hooked."

Susannah settled back into the cushions, enjoying the sun, the cloudless sky, the cool wind on her face. For the first time in a week she felt really happy. Was it the setting or the company?

As if he were reading her thoughts, Brett looked over his shoulder and gave her a rakish grin. She grinned back. But even as she did, a small part of her mind was still counseling caution. *Don't get too into this. You were going to play it cool, remember?*

A larger craft passed, sending waves slapping against the side of *Risky Venture*.

"You don't get seasick, do you?" Brett called out.

"You'll be the first to know if I do."

Susannah let the gentle throb of the engine relax her as the boat headed up the lazy, green river.

Forty minutes later she felt the boat slow and realized she'd dozed off.

"Did you have a nice nap?"

Susannah stretched and looked around. "I guess I did. Are we there yet?"

"Just about." Brett steered toward what Susannah realized was a smaller river whose mouth was almost hidden by trailing branches of willows.

"Are you sure we can get through?" Susannah asked as she ducked to avoid a leaf-covered limb.

There was a note of amusement in his voice. "Don't you trust me?"

"Should I?"

The boat nosed into a quiet little cove. Susannah took in the idyllic scene. "The forest primeval," she murmured.

"Umm-hmm. Only they're not towering oaks and hemlocks."

"Did you read Longfellow in school, too?"

Brett nodded and covered her hand with his.

For a moment they sat in silence. There was no sign of civilization here. Only water, giant trees and the sound of birds chirping in the branches overhead.

"I've never been in a place like this before," she breathed. "It's lovely. How did you ever find it?"

Brett cut the engine and sat down on the bench beside her. "I used to come here with my dad when I was a boy. We'd fish all day and then bring the catch home to my mom."

Susannah could see the memories meant a lot to him.

"Billy and I fish here. But we have to do the cleaning and cooking ourselves."

"Don't look at me."

"Don't worry. Your prize includes first-class treatment. In fact, this is extraspecial treatment. I wouldn't have brought just anyone to this place."

She'd forgotten the excuse for accepting Brett's invitation. "Then I'm honored." The words hung softly in the quiet of the cove. There was something about the spot that was intimate, like sharing a secret. "How is this place still so untouched?"

Brett pointed toward the far bank after dropping the anchor. "There's a marsh on the other side over there, so the developers haven't been able to get their hooks into it."

"I'm glad." Her voice was still low. Now she made a deliberate effort to break the intensity of her tone. "What's for lunch?"

Brett didn't comment on her attempt to lighten the mood. Instead he opened the picnic basket. "Let's see."

Jimmy Bob had packed a serviceable meal. Turkey sandwiches. Carrot and celery sticks. Fresh peaches.

"I have the feeling you gave him some pointers," Susannah commented as she munched on a carrot stick.

"Either that or he's been listening to your radio program on the sly."

"All right, you don't have to tell."

After they finished, Brett got out the fishing rods. "Ready for a lesson?"

"As ready as I'll ever be. Are you sure you want to go through with this?"

He leaned back against a cushion. "Let me tell you a little bit about fishing."

Susannah bit back a grin. He looked like one of those homespun TV pitchmen about to sell her a box of whole-grain cereal.

"Some people think you go fishin' to catch fish."

"Don't you?"

"That's just part of it. The real purpose is to have a good time. Unwind. Get in touch with nature. Let the current wash away your tension. There's no pressure to catch anything. Especially the first time."

How often has he delivered this sermon to stressed-out businessmen? Susannah wondered. But she had to admit she did feel wonderfully mellow.

"The middle of the afternoon isn't really the best time to catch bass, anyway," Brett continued as he pulled out a tackle box from under the bench.

"Are they taking a nap?"

"Not exactly. But they're most active in the early morning and in the evening."

"How come?"

"Because the little fish they like to eat feel safest in the shadows."

"I didn't realize there was so much to learn."

"And you haven't even gotten to the subject of bait."

"Could we just pass on that?"

"Can't get you interested in worms?"

She grimaced.

"I was going to do it for you."

She averted her eyes while he baited a hook.

"Okay, you can turn around now."

Susannah saw that he was holding one rod and had laid the other across the cushions. "An overhead cast is the safest for two people fishing from the same boat. It's also physically the most natural movement."

"You'd better show me."

"I intend to."

She watched him demonstrate the technique several times with his own rod. Then he pulled her to her feet. "Let's try it together."

He came up behind her and circled her waist with his arms. For a moment fishing was the farthest thing from her mind. Her senses were filled with things like the erotic tickle of his hair-roughened arms against hers and the solid impression that his hard chest made against her back.

She gulped. "Is this your usual technique?"

"It just gets better, sugar." She caught the half-teasing, half-cocky note in his voice.

"Fishing, Tanner. Let's get our minds back on business."

"Oh, had yours wandered?"

She didn't dignify the question with an answer.

For the next few minutes they practiced casting until she got the hang of it. Just as with any sport she'd tried in the past, Susannah found her competitive instincts roused.

"Not bad for a beginner," Brett approved. "If you want to practice at home, you can put an old tire out in the yard and try casting into it from thirty feet away."

"I might just do that."

He laughed. "Now let's make some hungry fish think your worm is swimming through the water."

After they again had cast their lines, they made themselves comfortable while they waited for the fish to bite.

"What do I do if a fish takes the bait?"

"With bass, you don't want to jerk the rod up with your arms. Just flick your wrists."

He had her try the motion until she got it right.

"Good," he approved.

Susannah was the first to feel a nibble. Her line jerked, and her eyes widened with excitement. "I think I've got something."

"Remember, just use your wrists."

Susannah was nervous and jerked too hard on the line. The fish got away. "Oh, sassafras." She looked at Brett in disappointment.

"Don't fret, honey. There's always more fish in the sea," he told her with a grin. "Actually, that reminds me of a story you might enjoy."

"Another of your stories. Is this about the one that got away?"

"Not exactly." Brett trailed his line in the water and settled back lazily against the cushions. "When I was a kid, I had a Labrador retriever named the Black Flash.

I just called him Flash. He had a talent for pulling fish out of the water when I caught them. So I taught that dog to go in and get them for himself."

"This is really a true story?"

He held up a hand with three fingers raised in the appropriate salute. "Scout's honor."

"Were you ever a Scout?"

"Well, I'm usually prepared."

She shook her head. "Go on."

"Anyway, our neighbors the Spaldings had this pond stocked with carp. One great old granddaddy carp was so big we called him king of the pond. There was this superstition that King had been there for a hundred years, maybe longer. If you caught him, you had to throw him back. One night when I was maybe about eight or nine, old Flash came home with King in his mouth."

"Oh, no."

"Oh, yes. And not only was the poor fish dead, it looked like old Flash had drug it through the mud. I knew I was in a heap of trouble." He paused for dramatic effect.

"What did you do?"

"I washed that fish off in the laundry tub." The corners of his eyes crinkled at the memory. "By that time he was really startin' to smell. So I sweetened him up with half a bottle of my daddy's best after-shave lotion."

Susannah bit back a laugh. "You didn't."

"It gets better. I took that old fish and threw him back in the pond. The next morning I heard Miss Spalding screaming, and I knew she must have taken the death of that fish badly. So I hightailed it over there to offer my condolences."

Susannah cocked her head expectantly and waited for him to continue.

"When she calmed down enough to talk, I found out why she was screaming as if she'd seen a ghost. You see, King had died of old age the day before. They'd even had a small memorial service when they'd buried him in the rose garden."

Susannah stared at him.

He nodded. "Flash hadn't pulled that sucker out of the water. He'd dug him up. You can imagine Miss Spalding's amazement when she found him floating belly-up, back in the water, like a phantom returned from the grave."

There was a moment of silence. Then they both started to laugh. When she could talk again, Susannah asked, "Did you tell her?"

"Yeah. I was afraid Miss Spalding was going to have a conniption fit, so I fessed up. You don't know how relieved she was to know it wasn't some supernatural visitation."

"Are you sure you haven't made this whole thing up?"

He was saved from answering by a jerk on Susannah's line.

"I got another bite!" she squeaked.

"Don't let it get away."

This time Susannah set the hook with the right pressure on the line, and the contest began.

Brett pointed to where the fish had broken the water. "It's a big one."

"I can feel that."

He came up behind her. "Want some help?"

"Not on your life." Following Brett's shouted directions, she battled with the fish. Finally she began to reel it in.

"More fish are lost at the side of the boat than any other time," Brett cautioned. As she pulled the bass out of the water, he leaned over the side with a net and scooped it up. "Got it!"

Susannah was so excited that she almost dropped the rod. "I did it. I did it. Wow. That's a big one."

"It sure is. Not as big as King, but respectable."

"But this one's real."

He ignored the suggestion that his story might have been more fiction than fact.

Susannah turned away when Brett unhooked the bass. He stowed it in an ice chest, then leaned toward the water to wash his hands.

"You look pretty proud of yourself," he said.

"I am."

"So am I. In fact, the occasion deserves proper congratulations."

"And what's that?"

"Well, if you were an Atlanta businessman, we'd break out ice-cold cans of beer. But I think we'll have to modify the custom a bit."

"Are you going to offer me a lukewarm diet soda?"

"No. Something with a bit more kick." He reached out and hooked an arm around her waist. His eyes were locked on hers as he slowly reeled her in.

Despite the teasing atmosphere, sensual tension had been building between them ever since Brett had stepped into the office at the marina. Now she softly breathed his name just before his lips took possession of hers. Like the fish she'd just caught, she was helpless to escape. The difference was that she didn't want to.

Wrapped snugly in his arms, she could finally acknowledge that two weeks estranged from him had been an eternity.

Eagerly her lips parted under his, and he growled his approval. The sweet invasion of his tongue in her mouth made her knees weak, and she had to cling to him for support.

She could feel the earth shaking beneath her feet. Then she realized that it was the boat that was rocking.

"Brett."

"Umm?"

"We're going to end up in the water."

He started to laugh. "You've made me forget every rule I ever learned about boating safety." Then he pulled her down beside him on one of the benches.

Susannah was thrilled at being close to him again like this. She leaned her head against his chest, listening to the steady pounding of his heart. His fingers gently stroked up and down her bare arms, sending little shivers through her, like the waves that lapped against the side of the boat.

"You don't know how much I missed you," he murmured with his lips against her neck.

"Yes, I do. If it was anything like the way I felt."

"And it was my damn fool fault."

"Brett, it wasn't just that I wanted to be with you. I felt so bad that you thought I would lie to you."

He held her tightly. "I should have known better."

For long moments they simply enjoyed the pleasure of discovering each other again. His lips explored her neck, the line where her hair met her face, her ear. Her fingers stroked across his shoulders and then slid upward to tangle in his hair. Finally he raised his head, and their eyes met. "Susannah, I've been thinking a lot about you and me."

"I have, too." Her voice was unsteady.

He cleared his throat. "I'm not going to be very good at this."

"At what?"

"Asking you to marry me."

Her eyes widened in shock. "Brett, I—I—didn't expect—"

He pressed a gentle finger against her lips. "Honey, don't say anything yet. Just let me speak my piece." He traced the outline of her lip with his index finger before he went on. "There have been lots of opportunities for me to get married again—if I just wanted someone to keep my house, warm my bed and help me raise Billy. But there was no one I really cared about enough to want to share my life with. Until I met you and fell damn near crazy in love."

Susannah felt her chest constrict. All along she'd been falling in love with him, too.

Her tender expression must have given away what was in her heart.

"Oh, honey," he murmured, then covered her lips with his again. This time it was a slow sizzling kiss that made her toes curl.

"Susannah, even after I started thinking about marriage, I kept telling myself it would never work, that you didn't belong in Silver Creek. But you proved me wrong again. You fit right in. It's not just me. Billy's crazy about you, too. Everybody in town is."

Susannah felt a knot of panic tighten her stomach. When he lowered his head to find her lips again, she pressed her hands against his shoulders.

"What is it, sugar?"

"Brett, your letting me know how you feel means a lot to me. It gives me the courage to tell you that I've been falling in love with you, too. But all this has taken me by surprise."

"Yeah. But when two people feel the way we do, they either live together or get married. And in a place like Silver Creek, it makes things a lot easier if it's the latter."

Susannah sighed. "I know."

"I asked you to marry me, not to jump into a swamp full of alligators."

She gave him a half smile. "I can't give you an answer right now."

"I'm not going to rush you. I just wanted you to know how I felt."

"I want you to know how I feel, too."

"How?"

"I can tell you better without words." She clasped her hands around his neck and pulled his head down to hers. Their kisses were punctuated with little sighs and indrawn breaths.

"Oh, Brett, I was so miserable."

"So was I, honey. So was I."

The shadows lengthening across the sun-dappled water wrapped them in the magic of the secluded cove. There was nothing but the two of them and the joy of being together once again.

Chapter Nine

The sun had set by the time Brett nosed the cabin cruiser back into the marina. After helping Susannah out of the boat, he slung his arm possessively around her shoulder, and they walked back along the dock. There was a cool breeze off the water, but being so close to Brett, she didn't feel the least bit chilly.

They were halfway to the office when he stopped. "Do you want your fish?"

"Oh, I forgot all about it." Susannah's brow wrinkled. "I don't think I want to clean it."

Brett grinned. "We'll save that for another lesson."

"Thanks."

He walked her to her car, and they stood for a moment listening to the chirping of the crickets.

"I'm glad you decided to collect your prize," Brett murmured.

"So am I."

"Then you won't get angry if I make a little confession?"

Susannah raised an eyebrow.

"I heard you were going to play bingo. So I sent that prize over with your name on it in case you won."

"You didn't!"

"I was desperate."

"But what if I hadn't won?"

"Then maybe the air-conditioning would have broken down in your exercise loft, so you would have had an excuse to call me."

"I'm always impressed by a man who's prepared for any situation."

"Yeah?" He took a step closer, sandwiching her between his body and the car. He placed his large hands on either side of the car top. "I've got you trapped."

She looked up and met his eyes in the moonlight. "But I'm a willing captive."

"Good." They kissed goodbye.

Susannah found herself humming a favorite old love song when she finally drove off into the night.

Over the next weeks Susannah spent a lot of time with Brett. They cooked the fish she'd caught one night for dinner. They sat in the back row of a movie, sharing a barrel of popcorn and giggling at a comedy that had finally gotten to Silver Creek. And, after the Fourth of July picnic, Susannah surprised Brett with several boxes of sparklers. She, Brett and Billy had a wonderful time with them.

The next week, they took Billy on a trip to Magnolia plantation. It was evident that the boy was all in favor of the way the relationship was going. In a way that made Susannah feel particularly good. But it also made her worry about how he would take it if things didn't work out.

As promised, Brett didn't bring up the issue of marriage again. But he put pressure on Susannah in a dozen little ways. He seemed to take it for granted that she was going to give him all her free time. And the way he talked about the future made it sound as though he was counting on the two of them being together.

Susannah began to feel as if she were on a boat being carried along by the current. She knew that if she didn't watch out, she was going to end up being swept along to the sea.

She was still grappling with her mixed emotions when an overnight special-delivery letter arrived from *Morning USA*. She'd forgotten all about the demonstration tape she'd rushed to finish before leaving Atlanta, but the network had been seriously considering her proposal all this time. Now they wanted her to come to New York to discuss a contract for an "Exercise of the Day" segment, which would air two or three times a week.

Her heart leapt with excitement as she read the letter. This was the kind of big break that came along only once in a lifetime. She wanted to rush over to tell Brett right away, but she had an aerobics class that afternoon. So she dutifully put her students through their paces. As she called out the steps and went through the routine, part of her mind was thinking about the offer—and about Brett. She'd worked hard to get where she was, and she'd always enjoyed her success. Now it was great to be able to share this wonderful news with someone who meant a lot to her.

As soon as the class was over, she called him. "I've got something exciting to tell you," she bubbled.

"You do?"

"Why don't you come over to dinner, and we'll talk about it then."

"Sounds good. Should I bring champagne?"

"That would be great! But let me stop off at the grocery store and get something special. I'll see you around six."

She splurged on veal, a bottle of Marsala wine to cook it in, fresh asparagus and new potatoes. By the time Brett came over, she had washed her hair, showered and slipped into an ice-blue shift that was a little dressier than what she usually wore. When Brett arrived, she was just rinsing the asparagus.

He set down the bottle of French champagne and gave her a quick kiss. Then he stepped back to admire her radiant smile. "You do look excited. What have you got to tell me?"

"This." She brought out the letter from *Morning USA*.

Brett looked a bit mystified as he took the piece of paper from her. Sitting down at the table, he began to read. She could see his brow furrowing, but he didn't say anything.

"What do you think?"

Still nothing.

"Aren't you excited for me?"

"Did you think I would be?" His voice was stony.

"Of course. I would be excited if you told me about a new business deal that meant a lot to you."

"That's different."

"Why?"

"Don't pretend you don't know."

"Are we having a communications problem?"

"Possibly."

Susannah could feel the blood pounding in her temples. "Brett, I've worked hard for this kind of break. Why don't you tell me why you're reacting like this?"

"Why? Okay, I'll tell you why. If you're so excited about this big news of yours, it must mean you've decided not to stay with me in Silver Creek."

For a moment she was speechless. She didn't know how to respond. "I hadn't been thinking in those terms at all," she said slowly.

"Maybe not on a conscious level."

"Brett, I told you I love you. But I didn't think I was going to have to choose between you and my career."

"Just what the hell did you have in mind? Were you planning to dance in here on the weekends and play house with me and Billy? That's sure not what I was thinking of when I asked you to marry me."

"That's not what I was thinking of, either."

"Then what?" he demanded in a tightly controlled voice.

"I—" She didn't know how to answer. She'd just crashed head-on into the problem that had been there all along.

"Well?"

"Brett, I... can't turn my back on this opportunity without at least going up there to talk to them."

"You know, the two of us keep having misunderstandings and patching them over."

"What's that got to do with anything?" she protested.

"Let me finish, if you don't mind. I kept telling myself that if we really cared about each other, things would work out. But this isn't just a little misunderstanding, it's a major point."

"I know that. I thought we could compromise. But now I can see that you won't be satisfied unless I completely cave in to your point of view."

"Now who's being unfair?"

"Well, what do you want me to do?"

"You wouldn't be content to run a diet-and-nutrition program in Silver Creek." It wasn't a question; it was a statement.

In response, her chin jutted up. "I might be. But I'd want to hear what *Morning USA* had to say before I settled for that."

"Settled for that! Listen, city lady, if you go up there to New York and they make you a good offer, you are going to take it. And to hell with me, my son or the town where I live."

"You certainly did put that in personal terms," she shot back, surprised by the vehemence of her own words.

"When a man goes so far as to ask a woman to marry him, he's usually personally involved."

She might have asked if they couldn't cool down and try to have a reasonable discussion, but when she looked up, he was opening the bottle of champagne he'd brought. As she watched in puzzlement, he took two mismatched tumblers from the cabinet and poured some of the bubbly liquid into each.

"What in the world are you doing now?" she questioned.

He held up a glass and pushed the other toward her. "Toasting your success. You deserve everything you get." He chugged down half a glass, then turned on his heels and strode out of the room.

Susannah stood there as the front door slammed. Then she picked up her own glass and took a swallow. The bubbles left an acid taste in her mouth.

She looked at the dinner she'd been preparing. She should put the food away in the refrigerator. But she couldn't face it just then. So she changed into jogging clothes. At this time of the evening it was still too hot to run. But she did anyway—until she was ready to drop.

The next morning, Susannah called the network. The argument with Brett had taken the edge off her excitement. But that helped her come across as cool and professional when she talked to Ed Dickenson, the *Morning USA* producer.

Ed was getting ready to leave with the production team for two weeks of filming in Europe. She waited while he checked his schedule. "I can work you in on Wednesday, if you can come up to New York," he said finally.

Two days was rather short notice. But in truth, Susannah was about ready to get away from Silver Creek. One of the women she'd been training to be an exercise instructor could fill in for her. So all she would have to cancel was a cooking demonstration at the grocery store.

"Can I call you back in a couple of hours?" she asked.

"I'm going to be in and out of the office. Just leave a message with my secretary."

After she'd taken care of her commitments in Silver Creek, Susannah made plane reservations, then called Ed's office to say she'd make the Wednesday appointment. The night before she left, Laura called to invite her and Brett to a cookout she was having because Bonnie's daughter and grandson were in town for a visit.

"I'm going to be in New York," Susannah told her friend.

"That's too bad. I know you'd like Carrie. She and I were best friends in high school."

"Maybe I'll get to meet her when I get back."

Laura's voice brightened. "Why don't you and Brett come over for dessert one evening next week?"

"Actually, you'd probably have a better chance of getting Brett there if I don't show up."

Laura clicked her tongue. "Oh, so it's like that again. For a while there it looked as if things were going to work out. But you two seem to end up fighting like pit bulls."

"Umm-hmm. Maybe I'm better off now that it's finally over." But her voice didn't really carry any conviction.

"Things might look better when you get back."

"I doubt it." Susannah sighed. "At least if you're still talking about my relationship with Brett Tanner." But she wasn't going to let the down mood carry over into her trip to New York, she vowed.

Travelling to her appointment turned out to be exhausting, and Susannah was glad she was in top physical shape. She had to run to make airplane connections in Atlanta. At JFK International Airport in New York, the baggage claim was a zoo, and the ride into Manhattan was nerve-racking. After the slow, easy pace of life in Silver Creek, the blaring of horns, screeching of brakes and near collisions left her heart pounding.

There wasn't time to check in at her hotel first, so she went directly to the midtown skyscraper that housed

Morning USA. As she stood on the sidewalk juggling her suitcase, briefcase and purse, an aggressive street vendor tried to sell her a silk designer scarf. She was pretty sure it was polyester. And she didn't need anything around her neck in the scorching New York heat anyway.

Ed Dickenson was younger than she'd expected for someone with so much power in the industry. While she sat in his office, the phone kept ringing and several assistant producers stopped in to ask for decisions on their material.

Finally he looked across the desk at Susannah. "Perhaps we'd better escape to Chez Etienne. I've left instructions not to be called unless there's a real emergency."

"It looks like you have your share of crises around here," Susannah observed.

"Welcome to the land of network TV."

The restaurant was only a few blocks away. As they made their way along the crowded sidewalk, Susannah wondered how anyone could take this sort of thing on a regular basis. Was this worse than downtown Peachtree in Atlanta? she wondered. Or had her perceptions changed that much in just a few months?

It was a relief to step inside the elegant little café Ed had selected and sit down at one of the beautifully appointed tables. Ed asked for a Scotch and soda. She opted for soda water with a twist of lime.

After they'd ordered lunch, he turned the subject back to the demo she'd sent in. "We had some staff take your tape home and try the routine," he told her. "They were all extremely enthusiastic."

"I'm glad to hear that."

"I felt the same way. And I pitched it to the front office. They've given me a green light." He paused while the waiter served them each a smoked-salmon appetizer. "Of course, with a new segment we always start on a trial basis and look at the ratings."

"Naturally," Susannah replied easily as she spread a piece of the fish on a triangle of bread.

"But we put out a lot of publicity—both in the print media and on the network. So we'd be giving you a good shot at it."

The more he talked, the better the proposition sounded. "We have great facilities here that you could use for the taping."

The offer gave her pause. "Would I necessarily have to do them in New York?"

"No. We have featured guest experts all over the country. They just have to be near a major production facility and get the material to us twenty-four hours before airtime."

"Then I could do it in Atlanta." But as she thought about going back home, she found herself picturing Silver Creek—and Brett. She pushed those thoughts from her mind. She'd come up here for an important purpose, and she wasn't going to let herself be distracted.

"Atlanta's fine," Ed agreed.

"And what would be my budget per segment?"

"Well, you understand we start new features at the low end of the scale."

She braced herself for some insulting offer.

When he came out with the figure, she had to stifle a gasp. Somehow she managed to nod noncommittally as she made some rough mental calculations. Even with production costs for three segments a week, her pay would be twice what she was making at Healthways.

"If that's not enough, I'm sure we can come to some agreement."

"I'll have to check on my actual costs."

Their main course came. Susannah's was chicken with dill-and-mustard sauce. It was good, but the sauce was a little high in fat. She found herself thinking about how she could recreate the same flavor with fewer calories.

"When would you want to start?" Susannah asked.

"We've found September is a good month to introduce new features," Ed replied. "A lot of people have the TV on while they're getting their kids ready for school, and our viewing audience jumps."

They went on to discuss other details. Ed wanted to begin with two segments a week and see how they were received.

"So could I tape six or eight sessions at a time?" Susannah asked.

"Whatever works best for you. But change outfits and freshen your makeup between sessions so it looks like a different day. We do that with the game shows."

The more they talked, the more Susannah was impressed with the setup. "Of course, I'd like to think about it for a few days," she told him. "And I'd need to have my lawyer look over the terms of any agreement."

"I'll have my secretary give you one of our standard contracts."

They returned to the office for the document, and Susannah left with a suppressed feeling of excitement. After checking in at the hotel, she was too wound up to stay in the room. She took a cab to one of the big department stores and spent the afternoon trying on fancy exercise outfits. She was going to need a lot of them if she took the *Morning USA* offer.

She bought several and started walking back to the hotel. On the way she passed an inviting little patisserie. A cup of tea would taste good about now.

When she opened the door, she was assaulted by the aroma of fresh-baked pastry. Maybe this once she'd splurge on something, like a strawberry tart.

As she sat down at a table, she thought about the offer from *Morning USA*. There was almost no doubt in her mind that accepting was the best thing she could do for her career. National exposure on the most popular morning show in the country. More money than she'd ever hoped she'd make. And a chance to help make millions of people's lives healthier. Who did Brett Tanner think he was insisting that she choose between him and something like that?

The nerve of the man. If he wanted a relationship where she didn't talk back to him, he could turn on the TV any morning and there she'd be.

The waitress came to take Susannah's order. She'd been intending to have something light. Instead, she found herself ordering chocolate cheesecake. She hadn't eaten anything that sinfully rich in years, but this certainly wasn't an ordinary day.

While she waited for the dessert, she kept thinking of more reasons why she was right and Brett was wrong. In this day and age, a man couldn't expect a woman to give up her career and stay home to take care of him. And he didn't have the right to expect her to change her whole value system just because she was in love with him.

A generous slice of cheesecake arrived. It was so rich that she started to feel full after only a few bites. Then she looked down at the plate. What in the world was she doing? *Trying to make herself feel better about Brett Tanner by indulging herself.*

She sighed and pushed the plate away. How many times had she told her health classes that out-of-control eating was no solution to life's problems?

As Susannah sipped her tea, the waitress kept glancing in her direction. Finally she came over. "Something wrong with the cheesecake?"

"It was very good," Susannah assured her. "But I'm, uh, on a diet."

"Then you shouldn't have bothered to come here."

The rude remark was a surprise. Over the last two months in Silver Creek, Susannah had gotten used to the friendly service everyone from the gas-station attendant to the cashier at the grocery store gave as a matter of course. Instead of coming back with a retort of her own, she just asked for the check.

It was rush hour by the time Susannah finished paying for the dessert she hadn't finished and stepped out to look for a vacant cab in the sea of cars that clogged the street. They were as scarce as hen's teeth. When one actually pulled up at the curb in front of Susannah in response to her upraised arm, a portly man jostled her out of the way, saying that he had to catch a train.

Shrugging, Susannah decided to walk. It was a hot, sweaty, twenty blocks. And the handle on one of the bags she was carrying broke. She was more than ready for the blast of cold air that hit her when she stepped into the lobby.

When she got up to her room, she looked toward the message light on the phone. Somehow, on the way back, she'd started hoping that Brett might call. But, of course, he hadn't. He didn't even know where she was, she reminded herself.

A long, cool shower washed away her feeling of fatigue. After wrapping herself in a fluffy robe, she climbed under the covers, leaned back against the headboard and picked up a pad and pencil from the bedside table. It was time to stop avoiding some serious soul-searching, she told herself. And because she was an organized person, it was easier to think with a pencil and paper in her hands.

Susannah divided the paper into two columns. At the top of one she wrote *Morning USA* in bold letters. It was hard to hold her hand steady as she wrote *Brett Tanner* at the top of the other. She felt something inside her chest contract painfully. She loved Brett. There was no use trying to pretend anything else. Coming to New York had made her realize how much she wanted to marry him and live with him and Billy in Silver Creek.

He'd been so insistent that his ideas about love and marriage were the right ones. And she had to admit that she agreed with him. What she resented was the way he'd issued an ultimatum. She could live with him in Silver Creek or pursue her career, not both.

Well, how important were each of the alternatives to her? In one column she listed all the reasons why her career was important. Satisfaction. Accomplishment. Helping people. Status. Being independent.

In the other she listed all the reasons why she wanted Brett. Love. Stability. Love. Fun. Affection. Love. Family.

As she stared at the paper, the words blurred and she realized that tears were brimming in her eyes. Several trickled down her cheek. She wiped them away with the back of her hand.

Drat the man. She loved him, and she wanted to marry him. But deep down she knew if she simply gave up everything she'd worked for because he insisted, she'd resent it. That would certainly affect the marriage for the worst.

But she also knew that if she just went back to Atlanta, she really wouldn't be content, either, having tasted the happiness of being with Brett.

She buried her face in her hands. Why did it have to be this way?

Maybe it didn't. Ed Dickenson had said she could tape several segments at one time. That would mean she'd only have to be in Atlanta a couple of days every few weeks. If she could find the right facilities in Charleston or Savannah, she could even do the tapings without having to spend the night away from home. Of course, that would mean giving up her job with Healthways, but she still could run a limited nutrition-and-exercise program in Silver Creek.

As the ideas began to solidify, she became more and more excited. There was no reason she couldn't have it all. Unless the rift between her and Brett was already so wide that it couldn't be repaired.

There was only one way to find that out—to confront the man.

Susannah folded her arms across her chest. The last time they'd had a misunderstanding, Brett had been the one to make the first move toward reconciliation. And, darn it, he should do it again now because this whole ridiculous breakup was his fault. Yet she knew in her heart that he wasn't going to. When Brett thought he was right, it took a lot to make him see the other point of view.

Her pride might suffer a little, but if she didn't give it a shot, she was going to regret it for the rest of her life. She wasn't a quitter. Even when Brett had been so set against her at the beginning, she'd gotten him to change his mind about the value of her fitness program.

When she got to thinking about it, she realized she'd gotten him to change his mind about a lot of things. She bit back a grin when she pictured him serving carrot and celery sticks at Billy's party. He hadn't made a big deal about the lunch he'd had packed for their fishing trip, but it was evident from what was in the hamper that he'd given Jimmy Bob special instructions about what to fix. And then there was the way he'd come around on the publicity issue.

Maybe there was hope for the man yet.

Chapter Ten

Because of the plane schedule, Susannah didn't get back to Silver Creek until Friday night. She'd planned to call Brett first thing Saturday morning. But when she actually thought about making the call, her palms started to sweat. Her whole future depended on how she handled him. And she needed all the advantages she could get.

Perhaps the best strategy was to bring over a peace offering. He really liked that peach crisp she made for him the night Jack had come to town. Maybe if she made Brett one now, it would help smooth the way for what she wanted to say. If things didn't work out, she could always throw it at him, she thought with a grim smile.

Susannah had all the ingredients she needed except the peaches. So she went to the grocery store, intending to just run in and make the purchase. But that proved to be impossible. The store was crowded that Saturday morning. Everyone she met wanted to tell her about all the excitement she'd missed yesterday.

Donna was the first one she ran into. "Did you hear about Bonnie's grandson?" she questioned breathlessly.

"Laura mentioned something about him visiting with his mother. What was her name?"

"Carrie," Donna supplied. "And her little boy's name is Tommy. That boy sure did give us a scare yesterday."

"What happened?"

"You know Bonnie lives out near the state park. Well, she was at the shop, and Carrie and Tommy were in the backyard."

Susannah waited for her to get to the point.

"Carrie went in the house to answer the phone. She was only gone a couple of minutes. But by the time she got back, Tommy was gone."

"Oh, my gosh."

"Carrie was nearly hysterical. She called Bonnie. And Bonnie called the radio station. Within twenty minutes there was a whole swarm of people out at the Childress place looking for the little tyke. Brett was the one who organized the search."

"And they did find Tommy?"

"Oh, yes. But it took till dark. They were tramping through the woods and calling for him, but he didn't answer. Carrie was sure some child molester had come into town and snatched him away; you know, the way you read about it in the newspapers."

"That must have been horrible for Carrie."

"But it came out all right in the end. Tommy had climbed up this outcropping of rocks and fallen asleep.

Brett was the one who thought to climb up there and look."

Susannah felt her chest swell with pride. Her man had saved the day. "So he's the town hero?"

"That's right. You ought to have seen Carrie throwing her arms around him and kissing him."

That didn't make her feel quite as good. Donna must have caught the expression on her face. "Brett and Carrie go way back. But she's married to a professional baseball player. That's why she was home visiting her mom. Because he's on the road."

Donna chatted for a few more minutes, and then she cleared her throat. "Heard you and Brett had another tiff just before you went up north for that business meeting of yours. By the way, how did that turn out?"

There was a time when Susannah would have been annoyed that her personal business was public knowledge. Now she knew it was just friendly interest. "Encouraging."

"Then you're, uh, going to be leaving Silver Creek at the end of the summer, after all?"

"It kind of depends on the town's local hero."

"Brett. Come to think of it, I haven't seen him since last night."

"Well, I'm sure I'll track him down."

Donna squeezed her hand. "I hope things work out for the two of you. I'd be mighty proud to have you stay in town."

"Thank you," Susannah murmured.

Before she left the grocery store, she'd heard the story three more times—with various embellishments. But in each of the versions, Brett had been relentless in his efforts to find the missing child.

"He told me Billy wandered off once when he was a little tot," Nora Mae related. "So he knew how panicked Carrie felt. Don't tell him, but Dwayne's going to give him a certificate of recognition."

If Brett didn't know by now, he was probably the only one in town who didn't, Susannah thought.

She was still thinking about the news two hours later as she took the baking dish out of the oven. She wanted to be able to bring him the peach crisp still warm, so she phoned the marina to make sure he was going to be there.

"Brett called in to say he was taking the day off," the secretary told her.

"Is he at home?"

"I don't know."

Next she tried his home number and got his son. "Hi, Billy. Is your dad home?" she asked.

"Miss Lindsey! You're back."

"Yes, I am. And I need to talk to your father."

She could hear the uncertainty on the other end of the line. "Well, uh, I'm not sure that's a good idea right now."

Her heart felt heavy suddenly. Had Brett left instructions for Billy not to put a call through from her? "Is something the matter?" she asked, making an effort to keep her voice steady.

"Dad would hit the roof if I told you," Billy whispered into the phone.

"You mean he doesn't want to see me?"

"He doesn't want to see anybody."

What could have happened? Susannah wondered. "Is he sick?" she asked.

"Kinda."

Now she was beginning to get worried. "I'm coming out."

"You'd better not. Listen, I gotta go. He's calling me again." Billy hung up without letting her ask any more questions.

She put down the phone and pressed her fingers against her lips. Brett was sick. With only Billy there to take care of him. Maybe he had the flu and couldn't keep any food down. Maybe he didn't want anyone to see him like that. But she couldn't just stand by and not do anything. She had to go out there. She'd take the dessert with her and put it in his refrigerator. She could heat it up when he felt better.

She'd thought about what she wanted to wear for her first meeting with Brett after her trip to New York. Now she didn't bother to change out of the navy slacks and white T-shirt she was wearing.

When she pulled in front of the Tanner house, she was alarmed to see Doc Crowley's Jeep parked in the drive. She took the stairs two at a time and threw open the door without even knocking.

The doctor was walking into the living room. When he saw Susannah, he shook his head. "That's about the worst case I've ever seen."

"Is he going to live?"

"He's not sure whether he wants to."

Susannah's alarm went up another notch. "What's wrong with him?"

"I reckon maybe he'd better tell you himself."

Without further prompting, Susannah set the peach dessert on a sideboard and flew down the hall. She almost bumped into Billy, who was coming out of one of the bedrooms with a bowl of chocolate ice cream. "I've never seen him say no to chocolate anything. But he won't even take a spoonful." The boy sighed.

"Where is he?" Susannah demanded.

"In there," Billy gestured over his shoulder. "But he's not in the mood for company."

Ignoring the warning, Susannah rushed into the next room. The shades were drawn and the room was dim. She looked anxiously toward the bed. It was rumpled but empty. "Brett?"

He didn't answer. She looked around and finally located him sitting in a straight chair by the window. Instead of reclining in the normal way, however, he'd turned the chair around and was leaning with the tips of his elbows propped against the back.

Susannah took a step forward and gasped. He was naked. No, not quite. He had on a pair of cotton briefs.

"Blast it! I told that boy not to let anyone in here except the doc."

She stared at him. It had been over a week since she'd seen him. Now, here he was with only enough on to save him from indecent exposure. Her gaze swept the broad expanse of his chest. The strong muscles of his arms. The red welts covering his body.

Susannah took a step forward, trying to get a better look. Almost every inch of skin surface was covered with the raw-looking blotches. Did he have chicken pox?

"It's not contagious, if that's what you're worried about."

"Oh, Brett, honey. You look so pitiful. What's wrong? Did you get burned?"

He muttered an expletive.

"Please. I want to help you."

"The last thing I need is some do-good city lady poking her nose where it's not wanted."

Billy had been observing the scene silently from the doorway. Now he entered the conversation. "He drug through a patch of poison ivy when he was looking for Carrie's little boy."

"When I need an interpreter, I'll ask for one," Brett said through gritted teeth. "Don't you have homework or something?"

"School's been out for two months, Dad."

"Don't smart mouth me. Get out of here."

Billy didn't need telling a second time.

Brett turned his attention back to Susannah. The belligerent scowl on his face almost sent her out of the room, too. But she stood her ground. He had the worst case of poison ivy she'd ever seen. The poor man must be really suffering.

Then she remembered the story he'd told her about the time he'd rubbed the stuff on himself to get out of school. Suddenly she couldn't keep the corners of her mouth from quirking up slightly.

His eagle eye didn't miss the tiny movement. "It's not funny," he spat out.

"I'm sorry." She instantly regretted her reaction. "I can see that you must be pretty uncomfortable. Did the doctor leave you any medicine? Is there anything I can do to make you feel better?"

Brett snorted. "I don't need anything from you." Then he tilted his head to one side. "What are you doing back in Silver Creek? I thought you were up in New York getting cozy with some big-time producer."

He *was* obviously itching—for a fight. Susannah wasn't going to let him bait her. "Actually, things went pretty well up there. But maybe we should talk about it when you're feeling better." She had come to the conclusion that he wasn't going to be receptive to anything she had to say while he was in this condition.

"You might as well entertain me with the tales of your success because I don't think we're going to be seeing each other much after this."

All the humor suddenly went out of the situation, and she felt a ball of ice form in her stomach. "You mean, if we don't talk this out now, I don't get another chance?"

"You're pretty quick, honey."

They stared at each other. She could see in the glacial depths of his blue eyes that he meant what he'd just said.

"Oh, all right," she began. "They, uh, want me to do two segments a week for *Morning USA*."

He stared stonily at her, and even though the room was cool, she felt a film of perspiration break out on her face. "They were really impressed with the tape I sent them. They're offering me national exposure. The chance to reach a whole segment of the population that needs to learn about a healthier life-style. And, uh, a lot of money."

"That's just wonderful for you, honey." His voice dripped with sarcasm.

Susannah took a step closer and knelt down beside him. She reached out to put a hand on his arm and then drew it back, remembering that he didn't want to be touched. "Brett, please stop twisting everything I say."

His lips twitched, and she braced herself for a sharp retort. But he didn't say anything.

"After they made me the offer, I thought a lot about what I really wanted out of life," she went on. "Sure, my career is important. But so are you—and Silver Creek."

"Sure."

She couldn't stop herself from reaching out and lightly touching his thigh. The warmth of his skin made her want to take him in her arms. From the very first there'd been such a strong physical attraction between them. If she could only use that now, maybe she could hug some sense into him. But that was denied her. "Brett," she said instead, putting everything she felt into the words, "there's no need to choose between the man I love and my career."

"I told you, I don't need a part-time wife."

She leaned toward him. "But it wouldn't be that way. I'd quit working for Healthways. I could tape eight or nine TV segments at a time in Atlanta—or maybe even Charleston. That way I'd only be away from home two or three days a month."

"And you worked all this out without even asking me what I thought."

That accusation was just too much. Here she was on her knees making all the concessions, and he still wasn't willing to meet her even a quarter of the way. She scrambled to her feet and glared down at him. "Brett Tanner, I don't remember you volunteering to help me figure out what to do," she shouted.

"Because I already knew it wasn't going to work out. The woman I marry isn't going to put her career first. Me and my son are going to be the most important things in her life."

"You are so arrogant!" It was lucky she hadn't brought the peach crisp into the room because she *would* have thrown it at him.

"I feel pretty bad already. I don't need insults on top of the worst case of poison ivy I've had since I was eight."

This was a no-win situation. Tears glistened in Susannah's eyes. But she wasn't going to let Brett see them trickle down her cheeks. In a very controlled voice she finished what she had to say. "I know you're feeling rotten. And you're obviously not capable of having a rational conversation. I guess the only thing left to say is that my contract in Silver Creek is up at the end of next week." She swallowed convulsively, and her fingernails dug into her palms. It was hard to admit how she felt when he was being so unreasonable. But she simply couldn't leave without trying to make sure that he understood what this meant to her. "Brett, I love you, and I want more than anything for us to be able to work this out." Her chin tilted upward. "But I'm finished begging. Unless I hear from you, I'll be leaving town next Saturday."

With that, she turned and left him sitting in his straight chair staring after her.

She needed to be alone. But as she hurried down the hall, Billy called to her. "Miss Lindsey, is it all right if I eat this peach stuff? I don't think my dad is going to want any. And I wouldn't want it to go bad or something."

She took a moment to get control of her features before turning to face him. "Sure. Go right ahead. Eat the whole thing."

"Thanks for taking care of my leg the other day. Even the scab is gone."

"That's good." She looked at him. He had the same blue eyes and sun-streaked hair as his dad. A sudden spasm clenched her heart as she realized that she wasn't going to get the chance to watch him grow up. "Billy, you're one terrific kid."

He flushed. "Naw."

"Yes, you are. And I know you're going to take good care of your father. If you need *anything*, call me."

"Dad wouldn't like that."

"I know. But I'll be here all next week if you need me."

He put out his hand in a very adult gesture, and they shook. "I'm going to miss you," he said solemnly.

"Me, too." She swept him into her arms and hugged him tightly, the way she'd wanted to hug his father. For a moment he clung to her just as fiercely.

The next few days were some of the worst—and some of the busiest—in Susannah's life. Her lawyer approved of the *Morning USA* contract—with a few minor changes that he planned to negotiate. The Cable News TV crew was back in town to film the progress Silver Creek had made during the ten weeks she'd been there.

In addition, since she'd promised to help the town continue with an exercise-and-fitness program after she was gone, she had to make sure several of her best students would be able to take over her exercise classes and cooking demonstrations.

The phones in her office and at home rang constantly. Every time they did, her heart gave a little lurch as she hoped to hear Brett's voice on the other end of the line apologizing for being so hateful. But he didn't call.

She heard through the town's efficient grapevine that he was back at the marina and that the worst of the poison ivy was over. Once, she even drove by. But she didn't go in. She'd made it clear that she wasn't going to make the next move, and she wasn't going to go back on that. She'd been as honest with him as she could be and said everything she had to say. If he couldn't see her side of things after he cooled down, then they didn't have a future together anyway.

Susannah spent Friday morning giving the Rollins cottage a good cleaning. While waxing the kitchen floor, she heard a car pull into the driveway. Her eyes fixed anxiously out the window. But it was Laura Henderson who climbed out. She had a bulky package under her arm.

Despite her disappointment that it wasn't Brett, Susannah was glad to see Laura. She smiled with satisfaction as she admired the success of one of her most determined students. Ten weeks ago Laura had been twenty pounds overweight. Now she was trim and fit. And she'd learned how to make the most of her dark good looks.

"I like that new outfit," Susannah complimented her. "Hot pink is definitely your color."

Laura grinned. "I've thrown out all my army-surplus tents—thanks to you and that color consultant we had down from Atlanta."

"So you're all set for your high-school reunion."

"Yup. Things have really worked out great. Your coming to Silver Creek was the best thing that ever happened to me."

"Don't give me the credit. Losing weight and getting in shape take a personal commitment. You did it yourself, girl. And don't you forget it."

Laura nodded. "I won't. I've gotten so I can walk past the Dairy Freeze without even taking a second glance."

"For that you deserve a combat medal."

Laura's face took on a pensive look. "I'm feeling so good about myself. I wish things had worked out for you the way you wanted."

Susannah swallowed. "I guess it just wasn't meant to be."

"I saw Brett, and he looks terrible."

"Good," Susannah couldn't help retorting.

"I'm going to miss you." Laura held out the package she was carrying. "I made you a little something to remember me by."

"How sweet of you." Susannah unwrapped the package. Inside was a beautiful hand-thrown cream-and-sugar set. "Oh, they are beautiful."

Laura smiled with pleasure. "If you don't want to put cream and sugar in them, you can use them for skim milk and artificial sweetener."

"Right."

They chatted for a few more minutes. "Well, I know you must have tons to do," Laura finally said.

"We'll keep in touch."

"And I'll watch for you on TV."

"I'm starting on *Morning USA* in September."

"It will be so exciting exercising with a celebrity."

Susannah laughed.

They hugged goodbye, and Laura climbed back into her car. Feeling sad, Susannah watched her back down the driveway. She wasn't just leaving Brett behind in Silver Creek. She had made a lot of friends here. Maybe she could find an excuse to come back and visit.

Dave Caldwell had arranged a special farewell broadcast of Susannah's call-in talk show, and on Friday evening, as she sat down in front of the microphone, Susannah was struck once again with the realization that this was the last time she'd be chatting over the air with the residents of Silver Creek.

"This has been one of our most successful programs," Dave told her. "At first people were a little shy about calling in. But they sure got into the swing of things."

The format, as usual, was a five-minute commentary by Susannah followed by fifty minutes of phone calls. Dave prescreened them to make sure no cranks got free airtime.

Tonight Susannah started off with a pep talk to keep people motivated to continue their good-health program on their own. "You've seen some remarkable changes in how you look and how you feel," Susannah told them. "And that ought to be reason enough to stick with the things you've learned. These are changes for life, not just for ten weeks."

When she finished, she glanced at Dave. "Well, I see we already have a call," she told the listening audience.

"You're on the air," Dave said.

"I don't have a question." It was Donna. "I just want to say publicly how much we all appreciate what you've done for Silver Creek. And for me personally. I didn't need to lose weight, but I sure benefited from your exercise program. I'm keeping up a lot better with the kids down at the day-care center. And my back doesn't hurt the way it used to in the evenings."

"That's great," Susannah told her. "If you're under a lot of tension, exercise does wonders." As she made the statement, Susannah wondered why it hadn't done all that much for her this week. Probably there was nothing that was going to affect her stress level—except time and distance.

Several more residents phoned in with testimonials. Then she saw Dave give her a strange look as he pressed the button for the next call.

"I've been listening to the folks tell you how much you've done for Silver Creek." The voice on the other end of the line belonged to Brett.

Susannah clutched the edge of her chair to keep from falling out of it. Was he going to bring their private standoff to prime time? Why had Dave cleared the call? He must know as well as everybody else in town how things stood between the exercise lady and the president of the Chamber of Commerce.

"And?" she managed to say.

"For some pathetic cases, ten weeks is just a drop in the bucket."

"I've made arrangements to help people carry on."

"Sometimes there's no substitute for personal attention."

"Brett, would you just get to the point of whatever it is you called in to say."

"I'm working up to it, honey. But this isn't easy."

The tone of his voice made her heart skip a beat. "Brett?"

"Have you ever heard that people who are sick sometimes say nasty things they don't really mean?"

"Are you referring to anyone in particular?"

"Oh, you know what I'm talkin' about, all right. That day when I was itching to death with poison ivy, I was meaner than a polecat."

"I noticed."

"But I've had a lot of sleepless nights to think about your proposition."

Dave's eyes widened.

Susannah remembered the radio audience. "It wasn't a proposition. I agreed to marry you."

Dave's voice broke into the conversation. "Then what's the problem?"

Susannah looked down at the console in front of Dave. Every light was flashing, which meant that there were over a dozen callers waiting to put their two cents in.

"She had this plan for how she could continue her career and still live in Silver Creek with me," Brett said. "And I was too stubborn to admit it would work. But the thought of her going back to Atlanta is like a knife twisting in my guts. Susannah, I love you. And I'm humbly asking if you'll still have me."

Her throat was suddenly so choked up she could hardly speak. "Oh, Brett, of course I will," she finally managed. "That's what I wanted all along." She heard a whoop at the other end of the line.

"You've just made me the happiest man in South Carolina. I won't take up any more of your airtime. But I'll see you after the program, sweetheart."

Dave began letting the other calls through. The airwaves were filled with congratulations and excitement that Susannah wasn't going to be leaving Silver Creek, after all.

Susannah sat there grinning and trying to sound coherent when all she could think about was Brett waiting for her.

When the program ended, she looked up to see him standing behind the glass panel in the studio door. The red blotches had just about disappeared from his face. And his rakish smile was back in place.

She threw open the door, and he put his hands on her shoulders and stared down at her. "I came close to making the worst mistake of my life," he said.

"I tried everything I could to get through to you. But it just wasn't working."

"Oh, honey. I know." He pulled her into his arms and clasped her in a bear hug that almost squeezed the breath from her lungs. She held him just as tightly.

Dave cleared his throat. "I'm getting ready to close up."

"Thanks for putting me on the air. I owe you one," Brett said, shaking the other man's hand.

"Just invite me to the wedding."

"We will," they assured him in unison.

As they left the radio station, Brett kept a firm grip on Susannah's shoulder. She could hardly contain her happiness. At last things were going to work out between her and Brett. But to her surprise, he didn't stop at his pickup truck or her car. Instead he led her down the sidewalk toward city hall until they came to the little park in the center of town. The summer night was warm and filled with the sweet scent of gardenias.

He dusted off a stone bench, and sat her down.

Susannah gave him a questioning look as he joined her on the bench. "Are you feeling all right, Brett? First you propose on the radio, now this. I'm afraid to even ask."

"This is a Silver Creek tradition—to seal a wedding bargain with a kiss in the town square."

"A bargain?"

"The tradition started a few hundred years ago when fathers used to get horses in exchange for their daughters' hands in marriage. A lot of fathers thought it was a real bargain receiving a couple of good workhorses in exchange for a daughter getting on in years."

"Brett!"

"Just teasing. Anyway, I guess we have struck a kind of bargain. You agreed to stay in Silver Creek most of the time, and I agreed not to be so pigheaded. I'm happy with my end of the deal."

"Me, too."

Brett's head lowered to hers, and Susannah met his lips with a kiss full of love and promise. When at last they pulled apart, she gazed into Brett's warm blue eyes and sighed contentedly. Brett Tanner and Silver Creek were going to be hers for keeps.

* * * * *

COMING NEXT MONTH

#652 THE ENCHANTED SUMMER—Victoria Glenn
When Derek Randall was sent to Green Meadow to buy the rights to the "Baby Katy" doll, he found himself more interested in rights holder Katy Kruger—a real live doll herself!

#653 AGELESS PASSION, TIMELESS LOVE—Phyllis Halldorson
CEO Courtney Forrester had always discouraged office romances at his plant. But Assistant Personnel Manager Kirsten Anderson was proof that rules were meant to be broken....

#654 HIS KIND OF WOMAN—Pat Tracy
As the widow of his boyhood rival, Grace Banner was certainly not Matthew Hollister's kind of woman . . . until a passionate battle led Matthew to a tender change of heart.

#655 TREASURE HUNTERS—Val Whisenand
When Lori Kendall became a contestant on a TV game show she discovered that the only prize worth winning was teammate Jason Daniels. But would Jason's secret send Lori home empty-handed?

#656 IT TAKES TWO—Joan Smith
As concierge of an upscale Montreal hotel, Jennie Longman was used to catering to her guests' eccentric whims. But Wes Adler had a request that wasn't in Jennie's handbook. He wanted her!

#657 TEACH ME—Stella Bagwell
When secretary Bernadette Baxter started teaching her boss, Nicholas Atwood, the fine art of dating, she was soon wishing she was the woman who'd reap the benefits of her lessons....

AVAILABLE THIS MONTH

#646 A MATTER OF PRIDE
Sondra Stanford

#647 THE MEDICINE MAN
Melodie Adams

#648 ROSES HAVE THORNS
Karen Leabo

#649 STARRY NIGHTS
Wynn Williams

#650 LOVING JENNY
Theresa Weir

#651 SILVER CREEK CHALLENGE
Amanda Lee